FARGO'S INSTINCTS FLARED

Once again a shadow flitted from boulder to boulder along the west rim, pacing him.

Fargo gave chase; whoever it was might pose a threat. His quarry wore a baggy brown shirt and pants and a brown hat that blended into the terrain, but Fargo would be damned if he would lose sight of him. The stallion swiftly gained.

Vaulting from the saddle, Fargo broke into a run. He was close enough to hear the rasp of the other's labored breaths and the *thap-thap-thap* of the other's shoes smacking the hard ground. Fargo poured on a last spurt of speed and slammed the Colt against the man's side.

Knocked off balance, the skulker careened against a boulder, cried out, and sprawled forward. His hat went flying.

Fargo cocked the Colt and pressed it against the back of the man's head. "Stay right where you are."

The man froze.

"Who are you and what are you up to?"

In a voice as melodious as music, the lurker replied, "Granny told me to hide until you were gone."

"I'll be damned." Gripping her by the shoulder, Fargo rolled her over. "You're female."

THE TRAILSMAN
#272

NEVADA NEMESIS

by

Jon Sharpe

A SIGNET BOOK

SIGNET
Published by New American Library, a division of
Penguin Group (USA) Inc., 375 Hudson Street,
New York, New York 10014, U.S.A.
Penguin Books Ltd, 80 Strand,
London WC2R 0RL, England
Penguin Books Australia Ltd, 250 Camberwell Road,
Camberwell, Victoria 3124, Australia
Penguin Books Canada Ltd, 10 Alcorn Avenue,
Toronto, Ontario, Canada M4V 3B2
Penguin Books (N.Z.) Ltd, Cnr Rosedale and Airborne Roads,
Albany, Auckland 1310, New Zealand

Penguin Books Ltd, Registered Offices:
80 Strand, London WC2R 0RL, England

First published by Signet, an imprint of New American Library,
a division of Penguin Group (USA) Inc.

First Printing, June 2004
10 9 8 7 6 5 4 3 2 1

The first chapter of this book previously appeared in *St. Louis Sinners,* the two hundred seventy-first volume in this series.

Copyright © Penguin Group (USA) Inc., 2004
All rights reserved

 REGISTERED TRADEMARK—MARCA REGISTRADA

Printed in the United States of America

Without limiting the rights under copyright reserved above, no part of this publication may be reproduced, stored in or introduced into a retrieval system, or transmitted, in any form, or by any means (electronic, mechanical, photocopying, recording, or otherwise), without the prior written permission of both the copyright owner and the above publisher of this book.

PUBLISHER'S NOTE
This is a work of fiction. Names, characters, places, and incidents either are the product of the author's imagination or are used fictitiously, and any resemblance to actual persons, living or dead, events, or locales is entirely coincidental.

BOOKS ARE AVAILABLE AT QUANTITY DISCOUNTS WHEN USED TO PROMOTE PRODUCTS OR SERVICES. FOR INFORMATION PLEASE WRITE TO PREMIUM MARKETING DIVISION, PENGUIN GROUP (USA) INC., 375 HUDSON STREET, NEW YORK, NEW YORK 10014.

If you purchased this book without a cover you should be aware that this book is stolen property. It was reported as "unsold and destroyed" to the publisher and neither the author nor the publisher has received any payment for this "stripped book."

The scanning, uploading and distribution of this book via the Internet or via any other means without the permission of the publisher is illegal and punishable by law. Please purchase only authorized electronic editions, and do not participate in or encourage electronic piracy of copyrighted materials. Your support of the author's rights is appreciated.

The Trailsman

Beginnings . . . they bend the tree and they mark the man. Skye Fargo was born when he was eighteen. Terror was his midwife, vengeance his first cry. Killing spawned Skye Fargo, ruthless, cold-blooded murder. Out of the acrid smoke of gunpowder still hanging in the air, he rose, cried out a promise never forgotten.

The Trailsman they began to call him all across the West: searcher, scout, hunter, the man who could see where others only looked, his skills for hire but not his soul, the man who lived each day to the fullest, yet trailed each tomorrow. Skye Fargo, the Trailsman, the seeker who could take the wildness of a land and the wanting of a woman and make them his own.

*The blistered land that would one day be Nevada, 1871—
Where the dead told no tales
and the living wished they were no more.*

1

The big man in buckskins caught up with the wagon train a week after he struck its trail. From a rise, Skye Fargo watched the nine wagons plod southwest across the alkali flats like so many canvas-backed turtles. A thick cloud of dust moved with them, shimmering in the heat haze.

Nevada Territory was like that. Hot and dusty and sparse on vegetation. An iron land, unrelenting and cruel, home to the hardiest of animals and some of the cruelest of men. It was no place for pilgrims bound for the promised land of milk and honey. Yet there they were.

Fargo's lake-blue eyes narrowed. He had spotted two outriders well ahead of the wagons. They were the only ones on horseback. Gigging his Ovaro down the slope, he matched their snail's pace. It would be dark in a couple of hours. That was when he would make their acquaintance.

Both Fargo and the Ovaro were caked with dust. His white hat was brown with it. He inhaled it when he breathed and tasted it when he swallowed. He wryly reflected that if dust ever became valuable, the few folks living in Nevada would be downright rich.

In the distance reared one of the more than thirty mountain ranges that slashed the territory from north to south. It didn't have an official name yet, to the best of Fargo's knowledge, although the old-timers sometimes referred to it as the Blood Red Range, after the crimson snow plants that pushed through the snow in the forests at the higher elevations.

A few prospectors had searched its peaks over the years but none ever struck it rich. The Northern Paiutes and the Western Shoshones both roamed the region. They were on peaceful terms with whites at the moment, although the army had received a recent report of a band of young Paiutes making trouble.

The piercing cry of a hawk drew Fargo's gaze to the sky. Other than lizards and snakes and rabbits, wildlife was scarce. He had heard coyotes yipping the night before. But he had not seen any sign of bears, wolves, or deer since leaving the vicinity of the Snake River.

Fargo figured he was far enough back that he would go unnoticed by the emigrants. Then a shout arose from the last wagon and was relayed up the line. Soon the pair of outriders were galloping to intercept him. As they came up he studied them from under his hat brim, and he did not like what he saw.

The rider on the right was as stout as a barrel and as greasy as bear fat. A Remington was strapped around his waist, and the hilt of a knife jutted from the top of his right boot.

The rider on the left was a runt with a chin that jutted like a lance tip and a nose shaped like a fishhook. He wore a Smith and Wesson. On his head was a raccoon hat that had seen better days.

Neither had taken a bath in a month of Sundays. They were filthy, their clothes were filthy, their saddles were filthy. They reined up twenty feet away and the stout one raised his hand. "Hold it right there, mister."

Fargo kept riding slowly toward them. He had the reins in his left hand and his right hand on his hip, inches from his Colt.

"Didn't you hear Swink?" the runt barked. "He told you to halt and you'd damned well better listen."

Fargo did not say anything. Nor did he stop. He focused on their gun hands, waiting for a telltale twitch or the jerk of an elbow.

Swink reined his horse so it was directly in the Ovaro's path. "By God, you'll do as we say. Ain't that right, Raskum?"

"It sure is," the runt echoed.

The Ovaro was only a few feet from Swink's sorrel when Fargo drew rein. "Move," he said.

Swink and Raskum looked at one another and Swink responded, "Is your brain sunbaked? You're not going anywhere until you tell us who you are and what you're doing here."

"We're the pilots for those prairie schooners yonder," Raskum added, "and we don't want you near them."

Fargo leaned on his saddle horn. He had worked as a pilot on occasion, and he knew many of the professional pilots who made their livings guiding wagon trains from Independence, Missouri to Oregon Country or California. He had never seen these two before. "I'm not contagious."

"Huh?" Raskum said. "What the hell does a disease have to do with anything? We don't care if you've got the measles."

"He means there's no reason for us to keep him from going near the others," Swink explained.

"We don't need a reason," Raskum said. "We're the pilots. We can do whatever we damn well feel like."

Fargo reined to the right and started to go around

3

them. For a few moments they were speechless with surprise, then both reined their mounts and came up on either side of his pinto stallion.

"Mister, you must have rocks between your ears," Raskum snapped. "If you don't stop that nag right this second, I'm liable to wallop you over the head with the butt of my pistol."

"That's a good idea," Fargo said. His Colt was in his hand before either could think to stop him. He slammed the butt against Raskum's temple and the runt keeled from the saddle like a whiskey-soaked drunk and struck the ground with a thud. Spinning the Colt, Fargo pointed it at Swink. "Your turn. Unless you're more reasonable than your pard."

Swink's Adam's apple was bobbing up and down like a walnut on a wind-tossed branch. "Me? Hell. Reasonable is my middle name. If you want to join us a spell, go right ahead. But you can't blame us for being cautious. It's our job to make sure those people don't come to harm."

Fargo twirled the Colt into his holster. "You boys should pick a new line of work. You're not much good at this one." He rode on.

Swink quickly caught up. "You're mighty slick on the draw, stranger. Mighty slick. I never saw your hand move. Not many men are that fast. I don't suppose you're someone I might have heard of?"

Fargo changed the subject. "Are you just going to leave your friend back there?"

"Hell, I've wanted to thump him on the head a few times myself to stop him from flappin' his gums. He can jabber rings around a tree."

"One of those," Fargo said to keep him talking. The pair matched the description he had been given but they were only the first link in the chain.

"Sometimes we can't be too choosy about who we

partner up with," Swink commented. "And Raskum has his good points. He makes the best coffee this side of St. Louis, and he doesn't snore." Swink paused. "Do you have a handle or would that be prying?"

"I have a handle and it would be prying."

"Fair enough. Never let it be said I can't take a hint." He took the hint for all of ten seconds. "What are you doing in these parts? There isn't a town within hundreds of miles."

"I had to leave Salt Lake in a hurry," Fargo said. Which wasn't true. But he could hardly admit the real reason he was there.

Swink grinned. "I savvy. Don't worry. Your secret is safe with me. I've ridden a few high lines in my time and I know what it's like to have the law breathin' down your neck."

"And now you're a wagon train pilot?" Fargo tried to keep the skepticism out of his voice.

"Heh. Let's just say things aren't always what we think they are and let it go at that." Swink looked back. Raskum was still serving as a fly stool. "Damn. I hope he ain't dead. I don't want to take these lunkheads the rest of the way by my lonesome."

The wagons had come to a stop. Men, women, and children were leaning from their seats or peering from the back of the wagons. A curly-mopped girl of seven or eight smiled and waved in greeting.

The drivers of the first two prairie schooners had climbed down and were waiting with rifles cradled in the crooks of their arms. One was almost as broad-shouldered as Fargo and wore clothes typical of a farmer: overalls, homespun shirt, and a short-brimmed hat. He was close to forty, his arms thick with muscle. The second driver wasn't more than twenty. Lean and gangly, he also bore the stamp of a tiller of the soil. A corncob pipe jutted from his shirt pocket.

The bigger man started right in. "Mr. Swink, who is this stranger and why have you brought him among us after what he did to Mr. Raskum?"

Fargo answered before Swink could. "He doesn't have any say in the matter. I do what I want when I want."

"Now see here." The big farmer gripped his Sharps in both brawny hands. "I'm the leader here, and I do have a say in things."

"No, you don't." Fargo swung down and walked to a water barrel on the second wagon. Without asking permission he opened it, lowered the dipper in, and treated himself to a swallow.

"That's my water," the young farmer said.

"*Our* water," someone corrected him, and a young woman swung from the seat and put her hands on her hips and glared at Fargo. She had fine blond hair done up in a bun and blue eyes that flashed with anger. "And I'll thank you, whoever you are, not to drink any without our permission."

Fargo took another swallow while admiring the swell of her bosom and the flair of her thighs. "The name is Flint."

"Well, Mr. Flint, you have some gall riding in here like this," the woman declared. "If you're not careful, we'll send you packing."

"You're welcome to try." Fargo gazed the length of the wagon train. The little girl in the last wagon waved again. "You folks sure are off the beaten path."

"We're taking a shortcut—," the young man began, and was immediately hushed by the older one.

"It's unwise to confide our personal affairs, Jared. We want no part of Mr. Flint and bid him to move on."

"Do you have a name or should I just call you stupid?" Fargo asked.

The big farmer drew himself up to his full height.

"I'm Peter Sloane, of the Iowa Sloanes. Our family has been in this country since seventeen ninety-six. My grandfather came over from Belgium and was one of the first farmers in Appanoose County."

Fargo gave the dipper to the blonde. Her nostrils flared and she hefted it as if she were contemplating hitting him. "Maybe you should have stayed there. Where you're headed, there's no law and little water."

"Our pilots know every creek and water hole in these parts," Sloane said. "As for the other, we have plenty of guns." He patted his Sharps. "No hostiles or owl hoots would dare tangle with us."

Fargo could point out that their train was much too small for there to be any safety in their numbers. He could also point out that nearly every creek was dry at that time of the year and water holes were few and far between. But all he said was, "Some lessons are only learned the hard way."

"You'll be moving on now that you've had a drink?" Swink asked hopefully.

Fargo shook his head. "I'm going to keep these fine folks company a while." He stepped to the Ovaro to climb back on and spotted Raskum galloping madly toward them.

Peter Sloane's cheeks had flushed and his knuckles grew white on the Sharps. "Now see here, Mr. Flint. We decide who can and can't join us. It's in the agreement each of us signed."

"I never signed it," Fargo said, placing his right hand on his Colt and his left hand on his saddle.

"Need I point out that you are only one man?" Sloane said smugly. "I daresay you will do as we want or suffer the consequences."

In a thundering cloud of dust Raskum drew rein and sprang to the ground. "You!" he roared at Fargo, glowering pure hate. "My head is splittin' because of what you did!"

"Look at the bright side," Fargo said. "You're still breathing."

Raskum's hand hovered over his Smith and Wesson. "No one does that to me! Do you hear?"

"You brought it on yourself." Fargo glanced from the runt to Swink and back again. Swink showed no inclination to lend his friend a hand. "But if you want to die, I'll oblige you."

Peter Sloane moved toward Raskum but stopped when Raskum shot him a savage glare. "I ask you to reconsider, pilot. This is no place for gunplay. Women and children are present."

"What do you know, you stupid potato planter?" Raskum spat. Any self-restraint he had was gone. "Out here a man has to stick up for himself or he's branded no-account. This peckerwood put a welt on me the size of a hen's egg and he has to answer for it."

Fargo had a decision to make. He would just as soon put a slug between Raskum's ears and be done with it, but the army was counting on him. Lives were at stake. Not just those of Sloane and his people, but those of emigrants who might come along the Oregon Trail next month or next year or the year after. Raskum was still glaring at Peter Sloane, so he took a quick step and planted his boot in the runt's groin.

Gurgling and grunting, Raskum clutched himself and tottered. "You—you—you—," he huffed.

Fargo slugged him on the jaw and Raskum sprawled face first in the dust and didn't move.

The farmers were rooted in shock. Peter Sloane's mouth opened and closed a few times but no words came out.

Bending, Fargo relieved Raskum of the Smith and Wesson and tossed it to Swink. "Hold on to this. Your friend will live longer without it."

Jared was in awe. "You whipped him without half trying."

"Violence is the last resort of the godless," Peter Sloane piously intoned. "Mr. Flint, you will leave, and you will leave this instant, or I will call all the men together and we will thrash you soundly."

Fargo stepped into the stirrups. "If anyone so much as lifts a finger against me, you'll be burying a lot of your own. Let's get going. There's still a lot of daylight left."

The blonde was fit to spit nails. "What do we do, Mr. Sloane? We can't let him boss us around like this."

"I'm afraid, Miss Fox, that for the time being we have no choice," Peter Sloane said. "This man is coming with us whether we like it or not."

Which was exactly what Fargo wanted to hear.

2

A sliver of sun was sinking below the far horizon when the pilots called a halt for the day in the middle of the vast alkali flats. Following Peter Sloane's lead, the weary teamsters formed their dust-caked prairie schooners into a circle. They unhitched their exhausted teams and strung ropes to keep the horses from wandering off.

Since there wasn't a lick of vegetation to be had, Sloane's people had to do without a campfire. They gathered in the middle of the circle, and after Sloane read a passage from the Bible, the emigrants ate a cold meal of jerky and stale bread and everyone was allowed to drink a dipper of water.

Fargo sat by himself, his back against his saddle, munching on pemmican. His Henry rifle was across his legs, the Ovaro dozing a few feet away. "I hope you have enough food and water left to make it wherever you're going," he broke the strained silence.

"What do you care?" the blonde responded hotly. She was seated next to Jared, her legs tucked under her, her shapely curves accented quite nicely.

"You're right, lady. I don't." Fargo played his part. "It doesn't matter to me if your skeletons are added to all the rest."

"My name, I'll have you know, is Cathy Fox. This is my brother, Jared." Cathy bit off a piece of jerky and chewed until her curiosity got the better of her. "What was that about skeletons?"

"The bleached bones of all those like you who thought they were smart enough and tough enough to make it to Oregon or California but who never should have left home."

"We'll make it," Cathy asserted. "Our water barrels are half-full yet and we laid up plenty of jerky and other food."

"Besides,"—Peter Sloane could not resist joining their conversation—"our pilots know this country like they know the backs of their hands and will keep us well supplied. Won't you, gentlemen?"

Swink and Raskum were a study in contrasts. Swink was happily wolfing jerky as if it were choice steak; Raskum was nibbling on his and glowering at Fargo. "Sure, Mr. Sloane," Swink said. "You won't ever have to worry with us along."

Jared Fox had not taken his eyes off Fargo since Fargo sat down. Something was on his mind. "Our pilots tell us that once we reach Barnes Trading Post, the worst will be behind us."

"Never heard of it," Fargo said. And he had been to every trading post between the Mississippi River and the Pacific Ocean. There were far fewer than in former years thanks to the drying up of the fur trade.

Swink was quick to say, "The post has only been in business about two years. It's run by a woman who calls herself Granny Barnes. She and her husband are the ones who discovered the Barnes Trail."

Fargo had never heard of that, either, which was strange given that he had crisscrossed the West more times than most ten men and was familiar with every major and minor trail to be found. "She did that in a buggy, did she?"

Raskum snorted. "A buggy wouldn't hold out fifty miles in these parts."

"He knows that," Swink said. "He thinks we're making it up."

Fargo had to remember not to underestimate Swink. The man's mind was sharper than his piggish appearance hinted. "Grandmothers don't generally break new trails through the wilderness."

"Granny was with a bunch of others," Swink said. "Pilgrims just like these. They were up along the Snake, halfway between Fort Bridger and Fort Hall. It was late in the season and they were afraid they wouldn't make it all the way before the first snows hit. So they struck off straight for California and stumbled on a new pass over the Sierra Nevadas. A short route that shaves two whole months off the trek."

"Two whole months!" Peter Sloane echoed. "Two less months of hardship. Two less months of deprivation. That's what sold me on the notion when we met up with these men on the Oregon Trail."

The comment perked Fargo's interest. "So they weren't your pilots when you left Independence?" It was added proof that Swink and Raskum were two of those he was after.

"We didn't hire one," Peter Sloane revealed.

Another man said, "Why spend the money when we were perfectly able to find our own way?"

"It's not like we can't tell east from west and north from south," Sloane tried to justify their mistake. "My pa taught me to use a compass when I was knee high to a cricket. I reckon I can find something as big as the Pacific Ocean."

Laughs and chuckles greeted his remark but Fargo wasn't amused. They were too confident, too cocky. They thought they could beat the odds, just as so many others before them, an attitude typical of those who never made it through.

"We were a mite skeptical when Mr. Swink and Mr. Raskum rode up and offered to take us by a shorter route," Sloane was saying. "But sixty days is a lot of time to shave off the trip. It's worth the fee they asked."

Fargo saw Cathy Fox frown. "I take it you don't feel the same way?"

"We're taking too great a risk. There are forts along the Oregon Trail for our protection. There's plenty of water to be had. Here, we're entirely on our own. If we run into trouble we might not make it out alive."

Raskum jabbed a bony finger at her. "You don't have much confidence in us, do you, missy?"

"Frankly, no," Cathy said. "You're not exactly an inspiring figure."

Raskum started to rise but Swink gripped his arm and shook his head. "That's all right, miss," Swink said. "We'll prove true. Wait and see."

Fargo was about to take another bite of pemmican when the small girl who had waved to him earlier boldly came up to him and stood with her hands clasped behind her back.

"Hi. I'm Mandy."

Fargo almost said his real name but caught himself and said, "I'm Flint. Pleased to meet you."

"I saw you hit the man with the big nose," Mandy said.

"He stuck it where he shouldn't," Fargo told her. "Did my hitting him upset you?"

"No. I was glad. I wish you would hit him again. I don't like him. He's always pestering my ma and it makes her sad."

Just then a woman came rushing up and scooped the girl into her arms. "That will be quite enough, Mandy. What have I told you about talking to strangers?" She glanced at Raskum, a trace of fear in her eyes. "And I hope you won't take what she said seriously, Mr. Raskum. You know how children can be."

"Nope, I can't say as I do, Sarah," Raskum replied. "I've never had any."

Mandy's mother was a beauty. Rich black hair cascaded to the small of her back, and she had an hourglass figure many women would die for. Brown eyes, high cheekbones, and full red lips completed the portrait.

"Has he been bothering you?" Fargo asked.

Sarah blanched and said much too quickly, "No, no, not at all. Mandy just gets silly notions from time to time. She was worse when she was six. She had an imaginary friend she talked to. Roger and I humored her but maybe we shouldn't have."

"Roger was my pa," Mandy said. "He's dead."

"You're heading for California by yourselves?" Fargo was impressed by the woman's grit but not by her common sense. The journey took months. A thousand miles and more across some of the most harsh terrain in North America, with beasts and hostiles a constant threat. To say nothing of long stretches, like this one, where there was no water to be found and precious little game.

"My sister and her family live out there," Sarah said. "She says the climate is wonderful and she can help get me a really good job."

Now Fargo understood. Jobs for women were few, and paid far less than men earned. Good jobs were rarer than hen's teeth. "I hope you make it safe and sound."

"You almost sound like you mean that."

Sarah turned to go but froze when Raskum said, "I'll be payin' you a visit later, widow lady, to talk about the mouth that girl of yours has on her. If you don't mind, that is," he added with a lecherous smirk.

Fargo waited for Peter Sloane or Jared Fox or one of the other emigrants to say something but no one did. Their expressions suggested they were afraid to, which put their relationship with their pilots in a whole new light.

Cathy Fox was studying him and trying not to be obvious about it. He noticed that while her lips were not as full as Sarah's, they were cherry red and heart-shaped. "Will you be parting company with us in the morning, Mr. Flint?"

"No."

His reply sparked a ripple of whispers and some resentful looks. Two who resented it the most were Swink and Raskum. Swink, the more intelligent of the pair, pretended to be interested in one of his boots so his feelings would not be as blatant. Raskum, though, glared and snapped, "Haven't we made it plain that we don't want you along?"

"And haven't I made it plain I don't give a damn?" Fargo took a last bite of pemmican and leaned back, lacing his fingers behind his head.

Raskum glanced at Fargo's Henry, then at the Colt, his gun hand twitching with the eagerness to kill. But he wasn't completely stupid.

"Have you been through this country before, Mr. Flint?" Cathy Fox inquired.

"A few times," Fargo admitted, "although not this exact area." With a casual wave of his left arm he encompassed the alkali flats and the mountain range.

Peter Sloane cleared his throat. "Mr. Swink was telling us there aren't any hostiles to worry about in these parts. You haven't seen sign of any, have you?" He glanced at Swink. "Not that I doubt you. But a body can't be too careful when it comes to those terrible red heathens. I lost an uncle to the Sioux."

"I've lived among the Sioux," Fargo mentioned, and almost laughed at their reaction.

Jared Fox was amazed. "Why didn't they lift your scalp? I've heard they hate our kind and want us rubbed from the face of the earth."

"Not all Sioux are the same," Fargo said, drifting back in memory to his youth. "The Oglala, the Mini-

15

conjou, the Hunkpapa, the Sans Arc, some hate whites more than others."

Peter Sloane muttered something, then demanded, "What have we ever done to them that they should take such perverse delight in massacring and mutilating us?"

"Besides kill their buffalo and their deer and other game? Besides take their land for our own? Besides build forts in their territory without their permission?" Fargo recited a list of Sioux complaints.

Peter Sloane sniffed. "You almost sound as if you sympathize with them."

"I do."

That shut Sloane up, but not Cathy Fox. "You're an unusual man, Mr. Flint. Are we to infer you hate whites as much as your Sioux friends?"

"I don't hate anyone unless they give me cause." Fargo pulled his hat brim low and settled back, thinking that would be the end of it, but Cathy Fox was a persistent young woman.

"What do you do for a living, Mr. Flint, if I may be bold enough to ask?"

Swink and Raskum, Fargo saw, were also interested, although Swink was smart enough to pretend he wasn't. "I wear out saddles."

Cathy grinned but promptly erased it. "I see. That's your way of saying it's none of my business. Then let me ask you another question even more pertinent in light of how you have attached yourself to us." Her eyes bored into the shadow under his hat brim. "Are you a killer, Mr. Flint? Or a violator of women and children?"

"The only women I violate are those who want me to," Fargo answered. "And yes, I've killed a few times."

The emigrants muttered among themselves and a

few women clutched their small children to their bosoms.

"How many times exactly, would you say?" Cathy pressed him.

"I've lost count," Fargo said. He wasn't one of those who carved notches in the handles of their pistols every time they bucked someone out in gore.

"I see." Cathy Fox considered that a bit, then said, "I hope you won't hold it against us if we want nothing to do with you. Take my advice and ride out at first light. We are peaceable people but there are limits to our peaceful natures."

"There are limits to mine, too," Fargo said, and rolled onto his side. He had no intention of falling asleep, though. Not until later. For now he contented himself with waiting for the emigrants to turn in. He doubted they would stay up late. Bouncing around in a wagon all day was more tiring than it seemed, and they wanted to get an early start.

Within half an hour only Cathy and Jared Fox and a young married couple by the name of Brickman were still up, talking about the heat and the dust and how glad they would be to reach California. Eventually they, too, headed for their wagons.

From under his hat brim Fargo watched the so-called pilots. Swink spread out his bedroll and was soon snoring.

Now only Raskum was still up, his arms on his knees, his scowl perpetually in place.

In the pale light of the half-moon, Fargo saw him inch his hand toward the Smith and Wesson. Fargo's own hand was close to his Colt, and he was set to draw when Raskum apparently changed his mind, rose to his feet, and swaggered toward Sarah Yager's prairie schooner.

Sitting up, Fargo quickly removed his spurs. Then,

as silently as a stalking Comanche, he glided across the circle.

Raskum was at the back of the wagon, staring angrily up at Sarah, who was in her nightdress and a robe.

"No," Fargo heard her say, "I won't take a walk with you. Not tonight, not ever. Go away."

"You won't want to rile me," Raskum warned.

"I'm not trying to. I just want you to stop badgering me."

"You've put me off long enough," Raskum growled. Suddenly lunging, he seized her wrist and twisted.

"Please," Sarah pleaded. "You're hurting me."

"I aim to have you, lady," Raskum declared, "and nothing on this earth will stop me."

3

Skye Fargo had a passion for three things in life: whiskey, cards, and women, although not always in that order. He had a passion for wandering, too. For seeing what lay over the next horizon. There were things he disliked with an equal passion: bigots like Peter Sloane, outlaws like Swink, and out-and-out bastards like Raskum.

Fargo never could stand to see others imposed on, either, maybe because he hated to be imposed on himself.

Violence was a fact of everyday life west of the Mississippi. Back east conditions were different. There, people could go where they pleased and do what they wanted with little fear of being molested or murdered. Here, law and order were largely unknown; there were too few lawmen to cover the many thousands of square miles of untamed frontier. As a result, thieves and killers and cutthroats of all kinds flocked there. Scum like Raskum, who thought nothing of forcing himself on a decent woman in front of her young daughter.

"Don't fight me, lady. You'll only make it worse for yourself." Raskum twisted Sarah's arm harder and she cried out.

"Ma!" Mandy screamed.

By then Fargo was there. Grabbing Raskum by the shoulder, he spun him around and slugged him in the gut. Raskum doubled over, his hand clawing for his revolver, and Fargo hit him again, a solid right to the jaw that crumpled him in an unconscious heap.

The commotion brought others on the run, the men with their rifles, the women rushing to help one of their own. They stopped short at the sight of Raskum lying on the ground with Fargo standing over him and Sarah with a hand to her throat and her other arm protectively around Mandy.

"What is the meaning of this?" Peter Sloane demanded.

"Three guesses," Fargo growled. Sloane and the other men knew Raskum had been bothering Sarah but had done nothing about it.

Swink shouldered through the emigrants and frowned down at his prone partner. "I keep telling him he should tend to business but he just won't listen." Swink bent to revive him.

"Leave him," Fargo said.

Worry marked Swink's dirty face. "Him and me have been together a good long while, mister. If you're thinking what I think you're thinking, I'd rather you didn't."

"Didn't what?" Cathy Fox asked.

Fargo walked around the wagon to the water barrel. He filled a dipper and brought it back and upended it over Raskum, who sputtered and coughed and then pushed to his feet livid with rage.

"You son of a bitch! That's the last time you'll lay a hand on me."

"It's the last time you'll lay a hand on a woman," Fargo said, handing the dipper up to Sarah. He slowly backed off half a dozen steps. "The rest of you might want to move out of the way."

"What are you doing?" Peter Sloane asked, then

blurted, "Oh!" and pulled his wife to one side. Others hastily scampered right and left. Jared Fox was practically beaming with eager anticipation but his sister was more puzzled than anything else.

Swink folded his arms across his chest to show he wanted no part of it. "This doesn't have to happen. I'll send him on ahead to the trading post so he's out of our hair."

"I'm not going anywhere," Raskum declared. "This tall drink of water has this coming."

"Just for once listen to me," Swink said. "You've bitten off more than you can handle."

"Thanks for the confidence," Raskum said bitterly. He hooked his thumbs in his gun belt, his right hand close to the Smith and Wesson. "How do you want to do this, Flint? On the count of three?"

"Draw any time you want."

"You're leaving it up to me?" Raskum sneered. "Do you know what that tells me?" He answered his own question. "It tells me that come morning, I'll get to piss on your grave."

Fargo did not say anything.

"You see, I've killed more than a few folks myself," Raskum bragged. "Maybe more than you."

"Please, gentlemen," Peter Sloane said. "Not here in front of everyone. What if a stray bullet claims one of us?"

"That hog won't wash a second time," Raskum said. He coiled his body, his hands at his side. "Let's get it done."

Fargo had met men like him before. Brutes who preyed on the helpless and weak. Bullies who did not care who they hurt. "Don't you want to slap me first like you did Mrs. Yager?"

"I'm warnin' you," Raskum hissed.

"I know why you picked her out of all the women," Fargo said. "She's the only one without a husband or a brother to stand up for her. And since she has a little girl depending on her, you figured she wouldn't dare lift a finger against you."

Raskum was close to the breaking point.

"Cowards are all the same," Fargo said. "Yellow through and through."

His gun hand twitching, Raskum hunched forward and snarled, "Not one more word."

"How about a string of them?" Fargo was calm, his body relaxed, his mind as sharp as a razor. "You're a maggot. A slug. You're what comes out of the hind ends of horses. The doctor should have dropped you on your head when you were born to spare the rest of us." Fargo could tell that one more insult was all it would take. "Have you ever been with a woman without paying her or forcing her?"

Raskum let out with a shriek of pure fury and swooped his hand to his Smith and Wesson. Jerking it from the holster, he thumbed back the hammer as it cleared leather.

Fargo's Colt was already out. It had leaped into his hand as if it were part of him. He fired, the impact of the slug punching Raskum backward. He fired again as Raskum swayed and tried to steady his aim. He fired a third time and Raskum was lifted off his feet and crashed to earth with his arms outflung. His body broke into convulsions but they lasted only a few seconds. Then there was stunned silence, except for the gasps of a few emigrants.

"You didn't have to do that," Swink reiterated.

"I'm not done." Fargo faced him. "Saddle up and ride. Your services as pilot are no longer needed."

Peter Sloane recovered his wits and bleated, "What's that you say? We paid him fifty dollars and we expect him to honor his commitment. We can't reach California without him."

"I'm your new pilot," Fargo announced.

"Preposterous," Sloane said. "We want someone who can find water and food, someone who has experience as a scout, someone who has done this sort of thing before." He paused. "What we don't want is *you*."

His smoking Colt still in his hand, Fargo asked. "Who wants to try to run me off?"

"Oh God," a woman in a pink robe said in fright.

"We can't let him do this," a man near her declared.

Swink was surprisingly unflustered by the death of his friend. He regarded Fargo with the same puzzled expression as Cathy Fox. "I suppose it won't do me any good to say you're making a mistake?"

"No good at all," Fargo confirmed.

"I'll drift, then," Swink said, "but it could be you haven't seen the last of me." Holding his hands out from his sides, he backed toward his bedroll.

The woman in the pink robe turned to Peter Sloane. "Do something! You're our leader. You can't let this happen."

Sloane gazed at the dark stains spreading across Raskum's chest. "If we resist some of us might end up like him."

Fargo stepped to his left so as not to lose sight of Swink. So far he had the situation under control but all it would take was for an emigrant or two to show some backbone and his plan would fall apart. But they didn't do a thing, and soon the clomp of hooves marked Swink's departure.

"I guess we should all turn in," Peter Sloane suggested.

"Not so fast," Fargo said. "A wagon train should always post guards at night. Each of you will take a turn for one hour. Everyone will be up by five, breakfast by six, and on our way by seven."

"But Swink and Raskum never had us post sentinels," a stocky man objected. "Why should we lose sleep when there's no need?"

"A small band of unfriendly Paiutes has been making trouble," Fargo said, "and there have been reports of people gone missing." He refrained from mentioning the army did not believe the two were connected.

"Hostiles?" the woman in pink said. "You're not saying that just to scare us?"

"You like Indians," Brickman said. "How do we know this isn't a trick?"

Sloane settled the issue. "We'll post guards like he wants. And to keep an eye on anyone else who might do us harm," he added with a meaningful glance.

Fargo inwardly grinned and made for the Ovaro. He checked the picket pin, then sat with his back to his saddle and began replacing the spent cartridges in his Colt. He heard footsteps but didn't look up.

"What I want to know," Cathy Fox said, "is what that was all about?"

"Raskum had it coming."

"I'm referring to *you*," Cathy said. "You're a walking contradiction. You rode up acting as mean as a kicked snake, then you save Sarah and warn us about the Paiutes. It doesn't add up."

"Don't make more of it than there is," Fargo advised. It would not do for her or anyone else to suspect the truth. He slid a cartridge into the Colt's cylinder. "Is there anything else?"

"Mr. Sloane wanted me to ask what we should do about Raskum's body. Cover it until morning and then bury it?"

"Leave it for the buzzards and the coyotes. They have to eat like the rest of us."

"That wouldn't be right. Everyone deserves a

decent burial. We would even bury you if it came to that."

Fargo liked her spunk. "I'll try not to inconvenience you." He gazed at the other emigrants. "The rules and laws these people live by don't apply out here. It's worth remembering."

"Decency isn't a rule, it's a way of life," Cathy responded.

"Not for those like Raskum who are always on the prod. Not for the Paiutes who are out for scalps. Tell your friends not to wander from the wagon train alone. Always go in pairs."

"There you go again," Cathy said.

"What?"

"Acting like you're a human being." On that note she left him.

Fargo replaced the Colt in its holster, then sat probing the darkness for sign of Swink. It was unlikely the fake pilot would return. Not alone, anyway.

Only after the last emigrant had turned back in and the man chosen to stand first watch was on a circuit of the circle did Fargo lean back and close his eyes. Sleep did not come easy. His gambit was fraught with peril, both for himself and the Sloane party. Saving them from their folly would take some doing, and might jeopardize his mission for the army.

Always a light sleeper, Fargo woke up each time the guard changed. He was also an early riser, and he was up well before any of the emigrants. Or so he thought. As he yawned and stretched, he glimpsed a face framed by blond hair watching him from the back of the Fox's wagon. He smiled, and Cathy ducked inside.

The next couple hours were busy ones. The men separated their teams from the other horses and drove them to their respective wagons. While they hitched the animals, the women were busy dressing the children and preparing cold breakfasts. Not much was said. They were a sullen, resentful bunch, who showed their feelings in the glances they cast.

After saddling the Ovaro, Fargo ate a piece of pemmican, then walked over to where the Sloanes and the Foxes and the Jurgensens were sitting. "It's not too late to turn back."

"How's that?" Peter Sloane said, a slice of bread halfway to his mouth.

"You're not that far from the Oregon Trail," Fargo observed. "And you'll be a lot safer taking that route than this one. In two weeks or so you'll be at Fort Hall. From there it will be easy. The tribes along the Columbia and in the Willamette Valley are friendly." Fargo had more to say but Sloane interrupted.

"But if we keep going, in a few weeks we'll reach the Sierra Nevadas, and once we're over them we're in California."

"It's dry as a desert until you get to the Sierras," Fargo noted. "You'll need every drop of water you have, and then some."

"We'll make it," Sloane confidently predicted. "We have complete faith in the guiding hands of Providence."

Fargo thought of the scores of pilgrims who had perished believing the same thing, but he held his peace. "As soon as you're ready, move out. Keep heading southwest." He decided to mount up and scout ahead a short way but he had taken only a few strides when he acquired a second shadow.

"You just did it again," Cathy Fox said. "For a coldhearted killer, you make a dandy Good Samaritan."

"If you all want to die, go right ahead."

"Sure, sure," Cathy said. "Maybe you've fooled the rest but you haven't fooled me. There's more to you than meets the eye, Mr. Flint, and I'm bound and determined to find out the truth."

Fargo came to the pinto and grabbed hold of the saddle horn and swung up. "There's something I'd like to find out about you, too."

"What would that be?"

"How you look without any clothes on." Fargo left her with her mouth hanging open, and once past the prairie schooners brought the Ovaro to a trot. He glanced back once, saw her staring after him, and laughed.

4

The morning was cool, the air crisp, but it would not stay that way for long. Fargo slowed when he was a hundred yards out and held to a walk. There was no sense in needlessly tiring the Ovaro.

Swink's tracks were plain. So were the ruts of the wagons that came this way before Sloane and his people. Exactly how many was hard to gauge but it had to be fifty or more, which tallied with the army's estimate of up to eighty.

In the past two years, four wagon trains had left Independence, Missouri, bound for Oregon and disappeared off the face of the earth. All four made it as far as Fort Bridger but vanished somewhere between there and the Dalles. There had to be an explanation, and since the federal government hadn't gotten around to appointing peace officers for that region yet, and since the army was stretched too thin to investigate, the higher-ups decided to rely on the services of someone they trusted. Someone who had done more scouting for them than any other. Someone whose reputation as a tracker was second to none. Someone who had done special work for them before, and always came through.

They sent for Fargo.

This time there was a difference. Thanks largely to the penny dreadfuls and newspaper stories about him and other frontiersmen, Fargo's name was fairly well known. He wasn't as famous as the likes of Jim Bridger or Kit Carson, but he was famous enough that the army wanted him to use a name other than his own. If foul play was involved, as they suspected, they were afraid the culprits would scatter for parts unknown if the outlaws learned he was nosing around.

So now Fargo was calling himself Flint. It went against his grain to playact but he would do it for the sake of those who had gone missing and for those who might disappear if he failed.

Already, Fargo had learned Swink and Raskum were involved. The pair lured small wagon trains off the Oregon Trail with their story of a new trail which could shave months off the long and arduous journey, an enticement few could resist.

Fargo had never heard of the Barnes Trail. The Oregon Trail, certainly. The Santa Fe Trail, the Mormon Trail, the Beckwourth Trail, of course. The Applegate Trail, the California Trail, the Cherokee Trail, it went without saying. But the Barnes Trail? No.

It was possible a new one had been discovered. Much of the West was still unexplored. It was even possible a new pass had been discovered over the Sierra Nevadas. But no one ever kept a thing like that a secret. Word of new trails always spread like a windblown prairie fire and soon everyone was using them.

The alkali flat stretched on forever. Fargo had to squint against the glare. He thought that Swink might circle around and shadow the wagons but Swink's tracks led unerringly toward the Blood Red Range.

Another hour, and Fargo headed back. It was best he stay close to the emigrants for their own sakes.

They had no idea of the dangers they were in for. He would scout again later, when they were closer to the mountains.

Fargo had mixed feelings about deceiving them. He would just as soon reveal who he really was and make them return to the Oregon Trail whether they wanted to or not, but Colonel McCormack insisted it was essential he keep his true identity a secret.

For the time being Fargo was stuck nursemaiding them. He would go on playing the part of Flint and hope the emigrants didn't get themselves, and him, killed.

The prairie schooners were lumbering along like giant overturned turtles, the blue of the wagon beds and the red of the wheels a colorful contrast in the bleak monotony of the alkali flats.

Fargo was glad the teams were horses and not oxen. The latter barely made ten miles a day when the terrain was easy, and this wasn't easy. Horses, on the other hand, could go a good twenty miles. But horses needed more water, and unless the Sloane party found some within the next day or two, they were in trouble.

Peter Sloane scowled as Fargo came riding back and swung alongside the lead wagon. "I was hoping you kept on going."

"You don't know when you're well off." Fargo gazed along the line, ensuring the wagons were properly spaced and that none of the animals were limping. "Any problems I should know of?"

"Everything was fine until you came along."

Every now and again Fargo had an urge to punch someone in the mouth. Such an urge came over him now but he disregarded it. "Are your people keeping their wheels greased?"

Sloane nodded.

The last thing Fargo wanted was for one of them

to break down so he also asked, "Did everyone bring a spare axle? And how about spare spokes?"

"How is it a mere vagabond like yourself knows so much about wagon trains?" Sloane asked. "But the answer is yes. I insisted everyone bring spares of whatever we might need. I'm not as worthless as you seem to think."

"Let's hope not."

"I sense that you don't like me very much, Mr. Flint, and the feeling, I will admit, is mutual. Think what you will of me, I take my responsibilities seriously. These people have entrusted their lives to me and I don't want anything to happen to them."

"Let's hope not," Fargo said again.

Sloane was confused. "You're a peculiar man, Mr. Flint. For the life of me I can't figure you out."

"Don't bother to try." Fargo reined up and waited for the second wagon to come alongside the Ovaro, then he clucked the pinto into motion. "Morning. Nice day if it doesn't rain."

Cathy Fox laughed. "When *is* the next rain due? We can stand to fill our water barrels."

"It won't be for another couple of months yet," Fargo said. "Not until September at the earliest."

Jared was beside her, his hat pushed back on his head. "I've never seen land so dry, so barren, so lifeless."

"I've crossed worse," Fargo mentioned. "Be sure to ration what water you have. Save most of it for the horses. When you get thirsty, stick a pebble in your mouth and suck on it. That helps."

"Any other tips you can give us?" Cathy asked.

"Go easy on the salt in your food. Once it gets hot, take turns handling the team and resting in the wagon. You won't sweat quite as much."

A gleam came into Cathy's eyes. "If I need to cool down I can always take off my clothes."

"Sis!" Jared exclaimed. "That's hardly proper for a lady. Must you always say whatever pops into your head?"

"Fiddlesticks," Cathy said. "I was only teasing our new pilot, just like he is always teasing us."

Something in the way she said it gave Fargo the impression there was more involved. "Take off your clothes in the daytime and you'll bake," he said matter-of-factly. "Unless you're used to it, like the Paiutes."

"These Indians you've talked about," Jared said, "are they on the warpath?"

"No. But there are always a few young warriors in every tribe who can't stand to sit in their lodges twiddling their thumbs."

"What will they do if they find us?"

"There's no telling," Fargo said. "They might run the horses off. They might take a few potshots. Or they might grab one or two of your women. Especially your sister."

Cathy began running a brush through her lustrous blond hair. "There you go again with your teasing."

"Indian men like hair like yours," Fargo said. "Among their own women light-colored hair is rare."

"I'm curious, Mr. Flint." Cathy paused in her brushing. "Have you ever slept with Indian women?"

Jared's embarrassment was worse than before. "That's enough! You'll have Mr. Flint thinking you're a loose woman."

"No more so than the next," Cathy said.

"What would mother think?" Jared scolded her. "She raised you better. And father would roll over in his grave."

It was unusual for a brother and sister to travel to California alone, sparking Fargo to ask, "Where are your parents?"

"Dead," Jared answered. "In a freak accident. They

were coming home from a church social late one night in a heavy downpour and their buckboard overturned. Father was going too fast, as he always did."

"He died instantly of a broken neck," Cathy said softly, "but mother lingered for weeks with her insides all busted. I was with her every minute right up to the end." A shudder ran through her. "I don't want to die like she did. I want my end to be quick and painless."

A sentiment Fargo shared. He would rather go out in a blaze of gun smoke or be ripped to pieces by a grizzly than spend his waning days in a rocking chair with drool dribbling down his chin. "Now you're out to make new lives for yourselves?"

"A good guess," Jared said. "Ohio holds too many painful memories. We want to start over, and we hear California is the place to do it."

"All we have to do is get there," Cathy remarked.

"Talk to you later," Fargo said, and wheeled the Ovaro. The Jurgensens smiled at him and Mrs. Jurgensen said good morning but the rest were clams. He brought the stallion up next to the last wagon and touched his hat brim to Sarah and Mandy Yager. "Ladies."

"I'm glad you came to see us." Sarah had her long black hair done up in a bright blue ribbon and wore a much nicer dress than the day before. "I want to thank you again for what you did last night, Mr. Flint. That man made a nuisance of himself from the first night they showed up. I was about at my wit's end."

Fargo shrugged. "I only did what needed doing."

Mandy had a green ribbon in her hair, and a doll in her lap. "Ma says that's the nicest thing anyone ever did for her, short of Pa."

"I was wondering," Sarah said. "If we can find some firewood, I would like to treat you to supper some night soon to show my gratitude. If you wouldn't mind, that is."

"I love to eat," Fargo said, and liked it when a faint pink tinge blossomed in her cheeks. "I was wondering something myself. Why is your wagon always the last in line?"

"It just works out that way, is all," Sarah said. "It takes me longer than the others to hitch my team so the rest always form up before me."

A twinge of anger spiked through Fargo. The last wagon was always the most vulnerable to attack. It also had to endure the choking clouds of dust raised by the others. "I have something to do," he said. A jab of his spurs sent the Ovaro to the lead wagon.

Peter Sloane glanced at him in surprise. "Is something wrong?"

"Starting tomorrow each wagon will take turns at the rear. Draw straws. Flip a coin. I don't care. But take turns."

"What brought this on?" Sloane asked.

"Your stupidity," Fargo said. "Another thing. When we stop at midday, find out who has extra weapons and who doesn't have any. Those with extra will share with those without."

"You can't force someone to share a gun against his will."

"Watch me." Fargo rode on ahead fifty yards and stayed there for the rest of the morning. He saw no sign of life, not even a lizard. When the sun was directly overhead he signaled for a halt. The emigrants climbed down to stretch their legs and have three swallows of water. It was all he would allow. Some grumbled but they did as he told them.

Fargo removed his bandanna and was wiping a thick layer of dust from the Ovaro's nostrils when shoes crunched and Cathy Fox said, "Do you make it a habit to help old ladies across the street too? Or are we special?"

"I'd do the same for any idiots in over their heads."

"I should be jealous. There's talk you're being extra kind to Sarah Yager. Strikes your fancy, does she?"

"She has her good points." Fargo noticed Sloane and Jared and the other six men huddled in the shade of the third wagon. From the look of things they were arguing about something. Him, probably.

"Such as?" Cathy asked.

"She doesn't wear a man's ears out with questions."

"Well, that certainly put me in my place." Cathy stepped closer, so close her breasts brushed his arm. "I can't help it if I've taken a shine to you. Women get a little green when that happens."

"Women get bossy when that happens," Fargo said. He shook the bandanna a few times and retied it around his neck.

Sloane and the other men had risen and were coming toward him. Each held a rifle. Over half had pistols. When Peter Sloane halted, so did the rest. Jared and Jurgensen hung back, clearly wanting no part of whatever they were up to.

"Want something?" Fargo asked.

"We've talked it over and come up with a solution that should please you as much as it pleases us," Sloane announced.

"A solution to what?" As if Fargo couldn't guess.

"To you. To your presence among us. To the fact we don't want you to pilot us."

"Speak for yourself," Cathy Fox said. "He's doing a better job than Swink and Raskum ever did."

"Hush, girl," Sloane said. "This is man talk. It has nothing to do with you females."

Cathy bristled and clenched her fists but Jared reached her before she could do anything drastic and pulled her to one side.

"I'm listening," Fargo said.

Peter Sloane glanced at the others for support and some of them nodded. "The solution is simple. We're willing to pay you one hundred dollars to leave us in peace."

"That's a lot of money."

"It shows how badly we want you gone. Do you agree?"

Fargo looked at them, then at Cathy and Jared, then down the line to where Sarah and Mandy were seated in the shade of their wagon. "Make it two hundred."

5

"Do you mean that?" Peter Sloane excitedly asked. "For two hundred dollars we'll have seen the last of you?"

A two-legged rake handle with a toothpick-thin mustache tapped Sloane on the shoulder. "I can't contribute more than twenty, Pete. You know that's about all the money we have left."

"That's all right, Nickelby," Sloane said. "I'm willing to make up the difference. Anything to be rid of this man."

"Show me the money," Fargo said.

Hands dived into pockets and delved under jackets and bills were thrust at Sloane, who counted them once and then counted them twice and grinned and held them out. "Here you go. Exactly two hundred dollars. We thank you for being so reasonable, and we wish you well."

Fargo took the money and folded it so it would fit in his pocket. "And I thank you. Now you can climb on your wagons and get ready to head out."

"But you're leaving," Sloane said. "We can head out whenever we want."

"I'm not going anywhere."

The emigrants thought he was joking. They looked at him as if he were joking. They waited for him to say he was joking. When it sank in he wasn't, they glanced at one another, uncertain what to do until Peter Sloane blurted, "But you agreed!"

"I didn't agree to anything except you giving me two hundred dollars," Fargo said. "If I left, you wouldn't survive a week."

Sloane sputtered in disbelief, at a loss as to what to say or do.

"You can't just take our money," Nickelby said. "It's the same as stealing."

Fargo placed his right hand on his Colt. "You're welcome to take it back if you want." He looked each of them in the face and not one of them would meet his gaze. "If not today, then tomorrow or the day after. I'll be with you a good while yet."

"This can't be happening," Brickman said.

"What will our wives say?" Nickelby brought up. "Mine will skin me alive for losing our savings."

Fargo turned to the Ovaro and mounted. "We're wasting daylight. I'll ride on ahead. Stick to the wagon tracks and we'll meet up at sunset."

Sloane was furious at being hoodwinked. "I demand you give our money back this instant! We will not be made a laughingstock."

"You don't need me to do that," Fargo said. "You do fine by yourself." He raised his reins. "Until sunset, gentlemen." The skin between his shoulder blades prickled as he rode off, and he half expected a slug in the back. But no shots thundered, and soon he was out of range.

The Blood Red Mountains had grown larger. Some of the peaks were eight to nine thousand feet high but that was nothing compared to the Sierra Nevadas where fourteen thousand was not uncommon. In the winter the high slopes would be covered with snow but now they were stark and bare. Lower down sparse timber grew.

Fargo figured the wagon train wouldn't reach the

range until the next day, midmorning at the earliest. He scoured the ground for tracks. Swink's still pointed southwest.

An hour later other tracks appeared. Those of several antelope, heading for the mountains. Soon afterward the tracks of two coyotes overlay those of the antelope.

The temperature, Fargo reckoned, had to be in the upper nineties. He longed for a stream or a spring so he could strip and jump in. For another thirty minutes he pushed on. Then, about to rein around and rejoin the emigrants, he drew up.

A rider had materialized out of the heat haze to the west. Was it real or a mirage? Fargo wondered. Blistering heat could play tricks on the mind. Once in Arizona he thought he saw a lake that turned out to be nothing but a sea of sand.

The rider was making for the mountains too. Suddenly he reined up and stared in Fargo's direction. Man and horse rippled like the pebbles at the bottom of a pool of rushing water. Details were hard to discern. The horse might or might not be a paint. The rider might or might not have dark hair and might or might not be wearing buckskins.

A Paiute, Fargo suspected. Either a lone hunter or one of the young warriors who tangled with an army patrol a month ago. Fargo raised his hand in greeting but the gesture was not acknowledged. After a while the warrior reined to the southwest at the same steady pace.

Fargo turned the Ovaro back the way he had come. The sun had set and twilight was fading to night when he spied the wagons already drawn up in a circle and the teams already picketed. He didn't see Cathy or Sarah. In fact, when he drew rein and swung down, he realized all the women and children must be in the prairie schooners.

Peter Sloane and four men were by Sloane's wagon, talking. Jared and Jurgensen were not among them.

"Where is everyone?" Fargo asked as he cautiously approached.

"The women are getting supper ready," Sloane said, his back to him. "The children went with them to get out of the sun."

Strange, Fargo thought, that he didn't hear a sound from any of the wagons. Even stranger, he didn't hear voices. "Are you sure you want to go through with this?"

"Through with what?" Sloane rejoined, and put the lie to his innocent act by turning and leveling a revolver. He and the others advanced.

"Is that for bluff or ballast?" Fargo asked.

"Neither." The men nearest Sloane moved to either side. "We've come to a decision, Mr. Flint. One you will not like but one which you will honor nonetheless."

Fargo could draw and fire before the farmer squeezed the trigger. Instead, he said, "Let me hear it."

"You will return our money. You will ride off and never return. Should you be foolhardy enough to come back, we will shoot you on sight." Sloane puffed out his chest, pleased with himself. "What do you have to say to that?"

"It's not what I say, it's what the Paiutes will do that counts."

"No, no, no," Sloane said, shaking a finger. "I seriously doubt there's a Paiute within a hundred miles."

"As near as three miles, as far as ten, depending on how far the warrior I saw earlier has gone," Fargo said.

Nickelby went as pale as paper. "You saw one? Actually and truly saw one? What was he doing?"

"Heading for the Blood Red Mountains. The same

range you're heading for. But don't let that worry you. You're not in any danger from one warrior so long as you keep your guns handy and guards posted. If he shows up with friends, well—," Fargo shrugged.

"You're lying," Peter Sloane said.

A single long step, and Fargo seized him by the wrist and wrenched, causing Sloane to cry out and drop the revolver. "I have half a mind to do what you want and leave," he said, kicking it out of their reach. "It would serve you right. But not the women and children. So you're stuck with me." He gave Sloane a hard push.

"I don't need a gun to make you leave," the big farmer growled. Balling his fists, he swung a looping right.

Fargo easily avoided the blow and brought his arms up as Sloane waded into him. The farmer was strong but Fargo had fought men far stronger, and Sloane was no fighter. His swings were wide and wild, thrown in desperation. Fargo blocked punch after punch but did not unleash one of his own until Sloane paused, winded from the flurry. Then he flicked a right, and when Sloane raised his arm to ward it off, he drove his left fist into Sloane's unprotected gut.

Peter Sloane doubled over, his face a beet, his veins bulging. Gagging, he took a couple of stumbling steps.

No one interfered. No one attacked Fargo. The others seemed surprised their leader had finally done more than flap his gums.

Fargo took Sloane by the shoulders. "Sit down. Bend over and take deep breaths and in a while the pain will go away."

Sloane angrily shrugged loose but did as he had been told. While he sat there wheezing and gasping, Jared and Jurgensen hopped down from their wagons.

"We didn't want any part of it," Jared said.

The women and children were climbing down, too.

Cathy Fox ran over and looked down at Sloane with her eyes blazing. "You wouldn't listen to me, would you? I'm just a woman and I don't know a thing, do I?"

Sloane opened his mouth to reply but all that came out was spittle, which dribbled over his chin.

Sarah was there, Mandy's hand in hers. "I agree with Cathy. I feel safe with Mr. Flint. Why can't you stop trying to get rid of him? Be reasonsable."

"Reasonable?" Sloane practically exploded. "The man forced himself among us, shot one of our pilots dead, took two hundred dollars of our money, and you want me to be *reasonable*?"

"He hasn't hurt any of us," Cathy said. "And two hundred dollars is about what you would pay an experienced pilot."

Sloane was about to burst a blood vessel. "Quit making excuses for him! He's a scoundrel of the first order and you're too blind to see it! He nearly killed me!"

Fargo hunkered so they were eye to eye. "If I had tried to kill you, you would be dead. We'll get along so long as you remember that you raise crops for a living, and I shoot people."

"How much more of you must we endure?" Sloane demanded. "How soon before we wake up with our valuables missing or have our throats slit."

Sarah came closer. "Now you're just being silly, Mr. Sloane. Would someone who saved me from a lecher like Raskum stoop to theft?"

Sloane jabbed a finger at Fargo. "None of us truly know what this man is capable of! One minute he's gunning a man down, the next he's giving us advice on how to stay alive!"

"That should show you something right there," Cathy said.

"All it shows me is that he's trying to lull us off

our guard. To lie his way into our good graces so he can turn on us when we least expect." Sloane growled like a mad dog. "You're entirely too trusting. You, and all the rest who think this ruffian is a godsend."

Fargo rose. "I'm not asking that you accept me. Or even that you like me. Just don't get in my way until I've done what I came here to do."

"And what would that be, Mr. Flint?" Mrs. Jurgensen inquired.

"I can't say," Fargo said, and let it go at that. He could not risk his secret getting out. To take their minds off him and what he was up to, he asked, "Do any of you have boxes you don't need?"

"Boxes?" Jared said.

"Anything made of wood you can part with. We need to get a fire going."

"In this heat?" Peter Sloane sarcastically commented.

"When was the last time you ate a hot meal? Any of you?"

"A hot meal!" one of the women said, clasping her hands to her chest. "It would be heavenly."

"And do wonders for our spirits," Cathy Fox said, giving Fargo one of her puzzled looks.

"Eggs will do since they cook up fast," Fargo said, "and any bacon that hasn't gone rancid." He went into his gruff act. "Don't just stand there, damn it. I'm hungry." Everyone scurried off except Peter Sloane, who stiffly stood and slowly shuffled to his wagon.

Fargo stripped the stallion and spread out his bedroll. By the time he was done the emigrants had a fire going. The women were cheerfully frying eggs and bacon while the men sat around staring at their sizzling suppers like so many half-starved wolves. He figured on helping himself after the rest had eaten but as he was leaning the Henry against his saddle, Sarah and Mandy came over, Sarah with a plate heaped with food, Mandy with a couple of slices of bread and a fork.

"I'll bring a cup of coffee as soon as it's ready," Sarah offered.

"Thank you." Fargo placed the warm plate in his lap and accepted the bread. "But you should eat before I do."

"You were out scouting most of the day. You need a good meal." Sarah gestured at the others. "Look at them. I haven't seen them this happy in weeks, and we owe it all to you."

Mandy placed her hand on Fargo's. "Mr. Sloane says you're a bad man but my ma says you're a good man and I believe her."

"Sometimes people aren't what they seem," was all Fargo would own up to.

Sarah smiled shyly and ushered her daughter back to the fire. Several times she gazed over at him, and if the meaning of those looks wasn't obvious to her fellow travelers, it was obvious to Fargo. He also noticed Cathy glance at him every now and again but her looks didn't hold quite the same promise.

Some of the emigrants inhaled their food. Others savored every morsel. Afterward, the men broke out their pipes and cigars while the women and children sat to one side, merrily chatting. Not Peter Sloane, though, who sulked through supper and then went straight to his wagon and was not seen again for the rest of the night. Mrs. Sloane did not go with him. She stayed up late with everyone else, talking and laughing.

It was pushing ten o'clock when they began drifting off to bed. By then the fire had died and the pans had been scraped clean and the children, Mandy among them, could barely keep their eyes open.

"I'll take first guard tonight," Fargo said when the

men were debating who should have the chore. He might as well, since he wasn't all that tired. That, and he said it loud enough so that Sarah heard as she was carrying Mandy off.

Soon the circle was quiet. All the emigrants had turned in. Snores rose from several quarters. The horses were dozing, and a nicely cool and refreshing breeze blew out of the northwest.

Fargo stood up and cradled the Henry. Time for his first circuit of the camp. He moved toward the edge of the circle.

Out of the dark stepped Sarah, her hands clasped behind her back. Nervously shifting her weight from one foot to the other, she whispered, "I thought you might like some company."

"You thought right," Fargo said.

=== 6 ===

Fargo liked how the starlight played off her long black hair. "Walk with me," he said, and moved beyond the wagons on the west side of the circle. Before them, like a great salt sea, stretched the alkali flats.

Sarah faced into the breeze, the lower half of her dress molded to her thighs. "I like it at night. It's so peaceful."

"Are you sure about this?" Fargo asked.

Her face was inscrutable in the dark. "There you go again. Thinking of me first. You flatter me beyond measure and I have no idea why."

Fargo put his hand on her hip. "It's not much of a mystery. I'm not a monk." He slowly ran his fingers down her leg.

"And I'm no nun." Suddenly embracing him, Sarah covered his mouth with hers in a kiss ripe with need and lust. Her tongue darted between his parted lips and swirled enticingly about his.

"Nice," Fargo said when they parted for breath. "Very nice."

"You must think I'm a hussy."

"You're a beautiful woman without a husband. You've been alone for too long and you want to forget for a while."

Sarah gripped his chin and bored her eyes into his.

"Who *are* you? How can you see into the depths of my soul?"

"I'm a good guesser," Fargo said. Which wasn't entirely true. Just as he had honed his skills at tracking until he was second to none, so, too, had he become adept at reading people. At seeing past what they said and did to how they truly were. More than once it had saved his life.

"There has to be more to it than that," Sarah said. "You're a man of marvelous mystery."

Fargo started to laugh but choked it off so as not to awaken the others. "I'm just a man. No more. No less. There's nothing special about me."

"In my eyes there is." Sarah ran a finger along his chin. "I will never forget you for as long as I live."

Fargo had no interest in hearing how wonderful he supposedly was. "Let's walk a little more," he suggested.

"I would like that." Sarah grinned and arched her back, the swell of her bosom adding to Fargo's growing hunger. "We can't go too far, though."

Fargo understood. She wanted to stay within earshot in case Mandy needed her. The alkali flats lay quiet and still under the celestial canopy but appearances were often deceiving. There was no telling who, or what, might be out there.

"I can't believe I'm doing this," Sarah said softly. "I'm not very bold by nature."

"Bold enough to gamble your life and your daughter's on reaching California."

"Necessity is the midwife to courage. I'm doing this more for Mandy than for myself. She has her whole life ahead of her and I want it to be a good one."

Fargo's arm touched hers—or did hers brush his?— and a warm tingle shot up it. The swish of her dress was a lure he could barely, for the moment, resist.

"We should reach Barnes Trading Post the day after

tomorrow," Sarah mentioned, "if what Swink and Raskum told us is true."

"That soon?" For Fargo it was good news.

"They said it's in a box canyon, cut off from the outside world by high cliffs. I always thought that was an odd place for a trading post."

Fargo thought so too. Normally, trading posts were built where their owners could reap the most profits, not off in the middle of a wasteland.

"There's water there," Sarah said. "A spring that never goes dry. Plenty of grass, too, they claimed."

"Did Swink or Raskum say anything else that might interest me?"

"Let me see." Sarah pursed her full lips. "Swink was fairly quiet most of the time. Raskum was the one who liked to hear himself talk, and he was always going on about something or other. One time he mentioned that we were lucky to be taking the Barnes Trail because in three or four years the trading post will close and no one will take it ever again."

Another odd comment, Fargo thought. Trading posts depended on trails, not the other way around. The people using the trail kept the trading post in business. If every trading post along the Oregon Trail were to abruptly close, thousands would still use the Oregon Trail every year.

"Raskum talked about how he was going to be rich one day, if you can believe that. He said he would have more money than he knew what to do with. Trying to impress me, I guess. It was the only time I ever saw Swink mad at him. Swink told him to shut up, or else."

"That's all?" Fargo had hoped for information that might explain the disappearances of the other wagon trains.

"Most of what Raskum said to me was personal," Sarah said, "and most of it was rude and lewd. Once he had the gall to tell me to my face that there would come a day, and soon, when I would beg him to help me and he would laugh in my face."

"Was he drunk?"

"Sober as could be. When I told him I would rather die than be beholden to him, he said they all felt that way until they learned different." Sarah paused. "What did he mean by that, you think?"

"Who can say?" Fargo responded, but he had a suspicion. He looked back. They had walked about fifty yards. Far enough, yet not too far. Stopping, he bent and placed the Henry on the ground, then unfurled and wrapped an arm around her waist and pulled her to him. She smelled of lilacs and soap. "You can go back if you want."

"No," Sarah whispered. "I've wanted you since the moment I set eyes on you. But I've never done anything like this before. Never been so impulsive. My husband courted me for a year and I still didn't give in until after we were wed."

His groin twitching, Fargo waited for her to make the next move.

"This is like a dream to me. I'm not sure it's happening, or if you are even real." Sarah searched his face. "Are you?"

In answer, Fargo grasped her hand and placed it on the bulge in his pants. She stiffened, and for a moment he thought he had gone too fast and she would pull away. Then her fingers began caressing him and his bulge became a redwood.

"Oh my," Sarah husked. "You're very well endowed."

Fargo kissed her. This time it was his tongue that slid between her lips and stroked her tongue in silken stimulation. She moaned and ground her hips against him, the fingernails on her right hand biting into his shoulder.

"It's been so long," Sarah breathed after a while. "So very, very long."

"Let's make up for lost time," Fargo said, and cupped her breast. He felt the nipple harden and pinched it, eliciting another, louder, moan.

"Oh yes! I like that."

Lowering his mouth to her neck, Fargo kissed and licked until she was squirming and cooing. When he squeezed her breast, she raised her face to the heavens, her mouth parted in an O. But she did not cry out. She was holding it in. She did not want anyone to hear them. She did not want her fellow emigrants to brand her a tramp. He squeezed her other breast and sucked on her earlobe and she squirmed all the harder, her nipples brushing back and forth across his chest.

Fargo began undoing her dress to gain access to her charms. She helped, as eager as he was for release, and when his mouth enfolded a taut nipple, she went rigid and her fingernails nearly drew blood.

"Yesssssssss."

Fargo lathered her left breast, then her right, sucking and massaging until both were heaving and her hot breaths fanned his neck. One of her ankles hooked behind his legs and she clung to his shoulders, her soft, scented hair spilling over his shoulders as well as hers.

"More," Sarah husked. "I want more."

So did Fargo. He hiked at her dress, pulling it above her knees, and delved his right hand under its folds. To his amazement she wore nothing underneath. Nothing at all. She had removed her undergarments in anticipation of this moment. His fingers brushed her velvet thigh and he stroked up one and down the other.

Now it was Sarah who was kissing his neck and nibbling on his ear. It felt as if her mouth had been forged in the molten core of a volcano. She rose higher to plant kisses on every square inch of his face.

Fargo caressed in small circles from her right knee to her downy thatch, and she shivered and nipped lightly at the sensitive skin on his throat. Extending his middle finger he slid it between her legs and let it rest on her moist slit.

"Ohhhhhhh," Sarah mewed. "I want you so much, Flint."

The mention of the name he was using jarred Fargo into glancing toward the wagon train. He mustn't forget why he was there, mustn't forget that two hundred and five people had disappeared. The night was tranquil, though, the prairie schooners were undisturbed.

Lowering his mouth to hers, Fargo sucked on Sarah's tongue while slowly parting her nether lips. He touched her swollen knob. For a few moments she was perfectly still, then she cupped him, low down, and did to him as he was doing to her.

"Don't stop," Sarah begged. "Please don't ever stop."

Fargo did her one better. Suddenly sinking to his knees, he parted her legs wider and nuzzled into her core.

"What are you doing?" Sarah asked. Then, "Oh! Oh! No one has ever done that to me before!" From her throat issued a drawn out groan that wafted on the breeze. Her hands fell to his head and she knocked his hat off and pressed his face hard against her. "Ahhhhhh. Like that! Like that!"

Fargo inserted his tongue and her inner walls rippled in response. He swirled it, relishing the taste of her womanly nectar, and suddenly she gasped and gripped his hair and thrust herself at him, gushing again and again. The lower half of his face became drenched with her juices. When he pulled back and rose, she sagged against him, spent.

"I've never," Sarah whispered.

Fargo stroked her hair. He would wait a bit. Pleasure, like good whiskey, should be savored, not rushed.

"Do you," Sarah began, but could not bring herself to ask the rest until he squeezed her arm in encouragement. "Do you think less of me?"

"Why would I?"

"What we're doing. A lot of people consider it wrong. We're not man and wife. We've only just met and here I am giving myself to you." Sarah placed her cheek on his neck. "I'm not the person I thought I was."

"You don't hear me complaining."

"I have no regrets, though," Sarah said.

While she was talking Fargo had freed his manhood. Bracing himself, he rubbed the tip where it would excite her the most, then gripped her hips and slowly fed himself into her.

The loudest groan yet fluttered from her, and Sarah threw back her head and closed her eyes. Her hands found his shoulders and she wrapped her legs around his waist, her ankles behind his back.

Fargo rocked upward on the balls of his feet and sank back down again. Settling into a rhythm, he felt her inner sheath mold to him like a scabbard to a sword. She matched him thrust for thrust. Her mouth was everywhere: his lips, his chin, his neck, his ears.

Their explosion was a long time coming. Fargo built up to it slowly, pacing himself. She went over the brink first. Her eyes widened and she mewed and then she exclaimed, "Again! I'm there again!" Her hips churned and her thighs clamped harder and she drenched him.

Fargo coasted to a stop. Sarah was breathing heavily, pure rapture on her face. Her arms relaxed and her legs grew slack. He gripped her hips as if to ease her off but instead rammed up into her with renewed vigor.

"More?" Sarah said in amazement, and after that she did not say anything for a long while.

A precipice loomed before Fargo. A precipice he had been over many times. His blood roared in his ears and he was slick with sweat. A constriction formed in his throat. Another moment, and the night spun, and he was swept along by a tidal wave of bliss. It was an eternity before he coasted to a stop.

They held on to one another until Sarah disentangled herself and smoothed her dress. "Thank you, Mr. Flint. I needed that."

"You have it backward," Fargo found his hat and jammed it on his head, then hiked at his gun belt to adjust it. The Colt started to slide out but he caught it and gave it a practiced twirl.

"My husband never liked guns much," Sarah mentioned.

"He never kissed you there, either," Fargo said, touching between her legs.

Giggling, Sarah pecked him on the cheek. "How did you get to be the way you are? To always do what you want. To not care what others think. To be the person you want to be and not the person everyone expects?"

Fargo shrugged. "I ride my own trail."

"I wish I could. But it's harder for a woman than a man. Anyone who says it isn't is a fool."

A slight sound reached Fargo's ears, a sound he could not quite identify.

"We should get back," Sarah said. "I don't like being away from Mandy. She's all I have in this world."

They linked elbows and strolled contentedly toward

the prairie schooners. Fargo could still taste her in his mouth, and her skin was a lilac bouquet. "Has Sloane told you about tomorrow?"

"What about it?"

"You won't be last in line, eating everyone's dust. From now on everyone will take turns."

"How did you manage that miracle?"

Before Fargo could answer, the night was pierced by a high-pitched scream of sheer terror. It wasn't the scream of a man or a woman. It was the scream of a child, of a young girl.

"Mandy!" Sarah cried, and flew toward the wagons.

7

Skye Fargo figured that Mandy had woken up, found her mother gone, and panicked. Kids her age did that. His main concern was for Sarah. The caterwauling was bound to wake up everyone else, and they would wonder what Sarah was doing up and about so late. Scooping up his rifle, he hurried after her, wishing Mandy would stop her screaming.

The next moment she did, only to cry, "Ma! Ma! Help me! He's taking me away!"

Then, just like that, the night went silent.

Fargo poured on the speed. The girl was in trouble. Real trouble. He overtook Sarah and streaked past her into the circle. Sloane and the other men were up, armed with rifles or pistols. Women were clutching children. He reached the Yager's prairie schooner and was about to leap onto the seat and check inside when hooves drummed in the dark and a forlorn cry wafted across the alkali flats.

"Maaaaaaaaaaaa!"

After that, nothing.

"What's happening?" Peter Sloane demanded, waving his rifle. "Was that the Yager girl?"

"Mandy! Mandy!" Sarah pushed past him and frantically climbed onto her wagon. "Little one? Where are you?" She was denying the evidence of her own ears. "Mother is here!"

Fargo ran to the Ovaro. He didn't bother with his saddle or the bridle. Grabbing hold of its mane, he swung up and rode bareback into the night. He hoped the child would cry out again or that he would hear the other horse but the only sounds were the ruckus being raised by the emigrants and the sigh of the wind.

When he was about where Mandy's cry had come from, Fargo drew rein and turned his head this way and that, straining his ears. To no avail.

Swinging down, Fargo searched for tracks. He might miss them in the dark but he had to try. Roving in ever wider circles, he was about to admit defeat and come back again at first light when he spied large pockmarks leading into the distance. Kneeling, he ran his hand over one. It confirmed his worst fear. The horse had not been shod.

As much as Fargo would like to go after her, he didn't. Tracking at night was slow and tedious. Even if he used a torch, it would take hours to cover ground he could cover much faster in broad daylight. Common sense, if nothing else, dictated he wait until morning.

Swinging onto the pinto, Fargo headed for the wagons. The emigrants were milling about. Sarah was by her wagon, her arms across her bosom, her head hung low. Fargo did not have to see her face to know she was in the throes of deep despair. Peter Sloane and several others surrounded her.

"I don't understand, Mrs. Yager," Sloane was saying. "What do you mean, you weren't here? Where were you?"

"I went for a walk," Sarah answered without looking up, her voice choked thick with emotion.

"At this time of night?" Sloane said. "What were you thinking? How could you leave your child alone?"

Fargo entered the circle and stopped the Ovaro next to his bedroll. As he slid down, the emigrants scurried over and immediately beleaguered him with queries, all of them talking at once.

"Where's Mandy Yager?"

"Why did you rush off like that?"

"What was all the screaming about?"

Fargo held up a hand to quiet them. He turned to go to Sarah but she was shouldering through them, tears glistening palely on her cheeks. She gripped him by the front of his shirt, her eyes asking the question she could not bring herself to voice aloud. "Mandy has been taken," he confirmed.

Sarah groaned and sagged.

"What do you mean by taken?" Mrs. Jurgensen asked.

"Kidnapped," Fargo made it clearer. He wanted to enfold Sarah in his arms and comfort her but it might bring more grief down on her shoulders. He had to be careful or he would compromise her.

"Who would do such a thing?" another woman wondered.

"Was it Swink?" Nickelby threw in.

Fargo told them the truth. "It was a Paiute."

Sarah groaned louder and her legs buckled. She would have collapsed had Fargo not caught her about the waist. Gently lowering her onto his blankets, he leaned her back against his saddle. She did not seem to notice. Her face had gone blank, her tear-filled eyes were wide and unfocused.

Peter Sloane had pushed through to the front. "How do you know the girl was abducted? Did you see her abductor?"

"I found tracks," Fargo said.

"Then why are you just squatting there?" Sloane demanded. "Shouldn't you be out after them?"

"It's best if I wait until dawn," Fargo explained. He

started to rise but Sarah clutched at his sleeve and leaned against him.

Most of the others were too stunned by the news to say anything. But not their leader.

"You were on guard, weren't you, Mr. Flint? How is it the child was taken right under your nose?"

Fargo had no answer.

"Your carelessness is beyond belief," Sloane would not let it drop. "You've gone on and on about the dangers we face in the wilds, and how we must always be vigilant, and now look."

"Indians are like ghosts," Jared came to Fargo's defense. "We can't blame Mr. Flint."

"On the contrary," Sloane said. "As he keeps reminding us, he's the one with all the experience. He should never have let this occur. If anything happens to that little girl, it will be on his shoulders."

For once Sloane was right. Fargo laid the fault at his own feet. Had he been doing what he was supposed to be doing, Mandy would be safe in dreamland. His neglect made it possible for the Paiute to waltz in and snatch her.

"Did you fall asleep, Mr. Flint?" Jurgensen inquired. "Is that how this terrible deed came to pass?"

"I just don't understand," someone else commented.

Fargo noticed Cathy Fox. She had not said a word.

"Maybe Peter had been right in wanting to run you off," Brickman said. "Maybe we should do it now and be done with you."

Sloane was quick to capitalize. "This is what comes of not listening to me! I've always had our best interests at heart, which is more than can be said of this killer. Let's throw him on his horse and rid ourselves of him once and for all."

"But what about Mandy?" a woman asked.

Tension crackled. Some of the men edged toward

Fargo. Then Sarah cleared her throat and said so softly they could barely hear her, "It wasn't Mr. Flint's fault. It was mine."

"What's that you say, Mrs. Yager?" Sloane said. "I didn't quite catch it."

A portrait of motherly misery, Sarah looked up. "Mr. Flint isn't to blame. I am. I should never have left Mandy alone. If you must point the finger of blame, point it at me."

"Where *were* you?" Mrs. Shaw demanded.

"How could you leave your daughter alone?" accused another. "What on earth were you thinking?"

Sarah broke into sobs of agony and buried her face against Fargo's chest. He would like to let her cry herself out but some of the emigrants were muttering among themselves. Placing his hands on her shoulders, he lowered her back down, slowly rose, and turned. "Proud of yourselves?"

Something in his tone prompted Peter Sloane and several of the others to back up a step.

"What did we do?" Sloane said. "You're the one who let the child be stolen."

"And you're the one who keeps rubbing *her* nose in it." Fargo pointed at Sarah. "Her daughter has been taken and all some of you can do is carp at her for letting it happen?"

A woman whose name Fargo didn't know sniffed in indignation. "She deserves to be chastised. We would never let it happen to our children."

"You're just lucky the Paiute didn't pick your wagon," Fargo said. Although now that he thought about it, he suspected the warrior had not struck at random. Odds were, the Paiute had been spying on them for some time and saw when Sarah went off with him. It might be the same renegade he saw earlier. Maybe the warrior had shadowed him back to the wagon train.

"You're sure there's only one savage involved?" Peter Sloane asked.

"No," Fargo had to admit. The one who took Mandy might be part of the band the army was after.

Cathy Fox finally had something to say. "What will they do to her, Mr. Flint? Surely they wouldn't—" She couldn't bring herself to say it.

"They'll probably take her back to their village and adopt her," Fargo said. They might do something a lot worse, something unthinkable, but for Sarah's sake, he held his tongue.

"So what now?" Peter Sloane asked. "Should several of us go after her once the sun is up?"

"I'm going alone," Fargo informed him.

"I don't know as that's very wise," Sloane said stiffly. "You've proven we can't depend on you. Why should we compound our mistake by leaving the girl's fate in your untrustworthy hands?"

The farmer would never know how close he came to being punched in the mouth. "Can any of you track?" Fargo countered.

No one could.

"Then you'll only slow me down. While I'm gone, the rest of you keep going. Follow the wagon tracks to the trading post. If you haven't found it in two days, make camp and wait for me."

"I insist at least one of us go with you," Sloane said. "For the mother's peace of mind, if nothing else."

Fargo glanced at Sarah but she was too devastated to comment. She was on her side, curled into a ball, her hands over her eyes, sobbing in great heaves.

"I'll go," Jared Fox unexpectedly volunteered. "If Mr. Flint will have me, that is. I'm the only man without a wife, and my sister can handle our wagon as well as I can."

Sloane frowned. "I suppose you are the logical choice. But I warn you to be on your guard. I'm aware that you hold Mr. Flint in high esteem. Just don't let your misguided respect result in an early grave." He raised his arms. "As for the rest of you, try to get some sleep. I will take the next watch to ensure we do not see a repeat of this horror."

They drifted toward their wagons. Some of the children were so upset they were weeping and sniffling.

Cathy Fox knelt on Fargo's blanket. "Sarah? You're welcome to spend the night with me if you want. You shouldn't be alone."

Sarah raised her head. "Who?" she said. Then, "Oh. Miss Fox. I would be grateful." She limply raised an arm and Cathy helped her to her feet and had her lean on her.

"Jared, you stay with Mr. Flint," Cathy told her brother.

Jared glanced at Fargo as if to ask, "Is it all right?," and Fargo nodded.

It was some time before the camp quieted. Peter Sloane marched around the perimeter, his rifle resting on his shoulder, military style. To the south a coyote yipped and was answered by another.

"Are they real coyotes or Indians?" Jared asked. He was still standing and seemed ill at ease.

"Real." Fargo stretched out on his back and tried not to dwell on Mandy. She must be scared to death. He remembered a girl taken by Apaches a few years ago. Although her father and friends rescued her, she was never the same. All the vitality, the life, had gone out of her, and all she ever did was sit in a rocking chair and stare at the walls. "Have a seat."

"These Paiutes who took her. They won't let us have her back without a fight, will they?"

"It depends on how much they want her," Fargo said. "Don't worry. We'll have surprise in our favor."

"I don't see how it's possible to sneak up on Indians. Their senses are so much sharper than ours."

"Yours, maybe," Fargo said.

"I wish I had your confidence. To be frank, the notion of hunting hostiles terrifies me. I've never fought Indians. I've never fought anyone. And I've certainly never killed anyone. I might not be much use to you."

"Then why did you offer to tag along?"

"Someone had to. Mr. Sloane wouldn't let it rest otherwise." Jared smiled. "On the bright side, I'm the one person you can count on not to give you a hard time. He was right about my respecting you highly."

Fargo responded, "There's not much to respect."

"You sell yourself too short, Mr. Flint. I would give anything to be as you are, to live as you do. To be free to wander where the wind blew me. To never be beholden to anyone."

"Is that important?"

"My pa always said that a man who crawls through life isn't much of a man. He never backed down to anyone, just like you. I've tried to follow in his footsteps but I'm not half as tough as he was."

"Get some sleep." Fargo pulled his hat low and closed his eyes. The last thing he needed was a pup lapping at his heels. He couldn't watch his back and Jared's both. "We have a hard day ahead of us tomorrow."

And there was no guarantee either of them would make it through alive.

8

Only two emigrants had spare horses and both were more used to the yoke of a plow than a saddle. Jared did his best to keep up but he had to constantly goad his mount, and he was not the best of riders.

The sun was an hour high. They were miles from the wagon train, the tracks so plain, Fargo could ride as rapidly as the heat allowed.

The Paiute had headed south at a trot, probably in the mistaken notion he would be pursued. When it became apparent no one was after him, he had slowed to a walk and held to that until he came to the foothills. Beyond, like stone ramparts, reared the mountains. Once among them, the Paiute bore to the southwest. Broken by ravines and canyons, they were a bewildering maze to anyone unfamiliar with their twists and turns.

"I sure am thirsty," Jared mentioned, wiping a sleeve across his profusely perspiring brow.

"Try not to think about it," Fargo said. Until they found water, their throats would stay parched.

"I don't see how anyone can live in this godforsaken country," Jared commented. "I wouldn't last a week on my own."

"It's not for greenhorns," Fargo said. In the wilds

only the strongest survived. The land was a harsh mistress, and nature exacted a fatal price for mistakes.

Jared squinted up at the blazing sun. "I never realized how good I had it back in Ohio. There's a lot to be said for civilization and its many creature comforts."

"So long as you don't mind living under someone else's thumb," Fargo said. They were rounding a crag. Suddenly they came on ruts scoured into the soil by the wheels of many wagons.

"What are these?" Jared asked.

"The wagon trains that came this way before yours." And not one, Fargo reflected, was ever seen again. He was watching the high lines for the telltale gleam of the sun off a gun barrel and didn't notice a new set of hoof prints until he was on top of them.

Four riders on unshod horses had come from the west and linked up with Mandy's abductor. They had talked a while, then headed deeper into the range.

Jared leaned from his saddle to study them. "How far ahead of us would you say they are?"

"Four to five hours."

"Then they could be anywhere by now," Jared said. "That poor girl must be beside herself with fear."

Fargo did not care to be reminded. He gigged the Ovaro on. Presently they reached the broad mouth of a boulder-strewn canyon hemmed by sheer rock walls hundreds of feet high.

"They went in there?" Jared apprehensively eyed the shadows. "We could ride right into an ambush."

Of more interest to Fargo was the flaring of the Ovaro's nostrils and the bobbing of its head. He sniffed the air himself but all he smelled was dust. Shucking the Henry, he levered a round into the chamber and entered the canyon. Ahead was a sharp bend. He was almost to it when he, too, caught the unmistakable scent of water.

At that instant, high on the west canyon wall, a

shadow moved. Fargo snapped the Henry to his shoulder and took a hasty bead but either it had been a trick of his eyes or whoever or whatever was up there had ducked from sight. He lowered his rifle and rounded the bend, and all else was forgotten.

A veritable paradise unfolded before them. Sarah had mentioned a spring that never went dry, and abundant grass. The spring was the size of a pond, the grass covered four to five acres. Trees also flourished, as did wildflowers.

"It's the Garden of Eden!" Jared exclaimed.

Fargo tore his eyes from the water and concentrated on the three log buildings: a shed, an outhouse, and the trading post. All were well built. A white sign with large black letters read: BARNES TRADING POST. Under it, in smaller print, was WEARY WAYFARERS WELCOME.

But the biggest surprise was the woman in a rocking chair on the porch. She had white hair done up in a bun and wore a freshly cleaned and ironed homespun dress. Spectacles were perched on the end of her nose. She was busily knitting and humming "Rock of Ages" to herself, and did not look up until they drew rein at the hitch rail. "How do you do?" she greeted them, her round, kindly, wrinkled face splitting in a warm smile. "Light and rest a spell."

Fargo saw that the Paiute tracks led right up to the same hitch rail, then the hoofprints went off up the canyon. "We're looking for someone," he brusquely announced.

"Heavens to Betsy," the old woman said, her hazel eyes twinkling. "You look fit to pin my ears back."

Jared started to dismount but Fargo glanced at him and shook his head, then pointed at the tracks. "A few Paiute ears will do. They stole a girl from a wagon train I'm guiding."

"Would she be a precious little eight-year-old bundle of joy who goes by the name of Mandy Yager?"

"You've talked to her?" Fargo said.

"Land sakes, yes. She about jabbered my ears off before she fell asleep." The old woman wagged her knitting needles. "Those ornery Paiutes should be strung up by their thumbs for what they did. But I settled for telling them to make themselves scarce or I would blow out their wicks." From under the half-done shawl in her lap she produced an old Walker Colt. "They knew I meant business."

"Then Mandy is here!" Jared declared.

"Isn't that what I just said, son?" the woman rejoined. "Use your head for something more than a hat rack."

Fargo was off the stallion and onto the porch in a lithe bound. He had his hand on the latch when the click of the Walker's hammer rooted him in place.

"Maybe you didn't hear me either," the woman said. "She's sleeping right now, and I would hate for her to be disturbed after all she's been through."

"I just want to make sure she's all right," Fargo assured her. "She knows me. We're friends."

"Says you. But I don't know you from Adam. So why don't we sit and have a nice chat while we wait for her to wake up?" The old woman trained the cumbersome Walker on Jared Fox. "The invite includes you, too. It's been a coon's age since I had company, and I do so love to hear the latest news."

"It hasn't been that long," Fargo said. "The Paiutes paid you a visit not long ago."

The woman's hazel eyes lit with amusement. "Your point being, I gather, that I must be a Paiute myself?"

Despite himself, Fargo laughed. "Not many settlers are friendly with renegades. I find it peculiar."

"Do you now?" the woman chortled. "Imagine those pesky Paiutes stopping at the only trading post to be found for hundreds of miles!"

Jared said accusingly, "You do business with them?"

"Sonny, I do business with anyone so long as they mind their elders." She placed the big Colt in her lap. "Now where are my manners? I haven't introduced myself." She bestowed another of those kindly smiles. "I'm Ethel Barnes. Grandma Barnes, my kin call me. Which I guess is why most folks have taken to calling me Granny Barnes." Granny smiled sweetly. "Who might you be?"

"I'm Jared Fox," Jared introduced himself, "and this is Flint."

Granny stared at Fargo. "Would that be your last name or your first name, tall, broad-shouldered, and handsome?"

Again Fargo laughed. "Both."

"How interesting. Your parents must have suffered from a deplorable lack of imagination or else they were powerful lazy."

Jared stepped onto the porch, leaned his rifle against a post, and sat in a chair. "I can't get over it, Granny Barnes. Meeting a nice lady like you in the middle of this awful land."

"Call me Granny, son. Everyone else does." Granny gazed out over her oasis of life. "I fell in love with this spot the day we stumbled on it. We were out of water, out of food. Our horses were skin and bones. Another day and we'd have given up the ghost."

"'We'?" Fargo said.

"My husband, George, and I. We were bound for California and had heard from an old mountain man about a shortcut. This was, oh, about five years ago. We made it to California, sure enough, but then George up and died on me."

"I'm terribly sorry to hear that, Granny," Jared said. "I know what you went through. My sister and I lost our parents not long ago."

"Yes, well, it was George's own fault," Granny said. "He never did have much willpower, and his weakness killed him, you might say." She began slowly rocking. "After I buried him, California didn't appeal to me any more. So I came back here and set up my trading post."

"All by yourself?" Fargo asked.

Granny twisted in the rocking chair and smacked the building. "Oh, sure. I chopped and trimmed and moved all these heavy logs by my lonesome." She chuckled. "I hired some men. Kept two of them on to pilot folks who might want to take the Barnes Trail." She fixed her hazel eyes on him, the light of friendliness fading. "You killed one of them, Mr. Flint."

"Swink has been here," Fargo said.

"Been and gone. He told me Raskum was trifling with one of the women and you shot him. Is that how it went?"

Fargo nodded.

"Well then, good riddance to bad rubbish. I never much liked Raskum but it's hard to get good help in these parts." Granny sighed. "And now Swink has pulled up stakes, too. You had him plumb scared, Mr. Flint. He says you're a natural-born killer." She paused. "Is that true too?"

"I've never been shy about squeezing the trigger when I had to," was all Fargo would say.

"And now you've taken it on yourself to pilot the Sloane party to California? How do they feel about it?"

"How they feel doesn't count," Fargo said.

"I see." Granny grinned. "You do what you want and everyone else be damned. Some folks might say that's wrong but I admire your sand. Too many men these days aren't fit to wear britches."

Jared had something else on his mind. "Granny, aren't you afraid living way out here by yourself?"

"I wasn't brought up in the woods to be scared by owls. At my age, there's nothing I'm afeared of. Not even dying." Granny patted the Walker Colt. "And I'm a pretty fair hand with this cannon."

"It's not like the Paiutes to give up a captive," Fargo mentioned.

"For a hundred dollars worth of trade goods they'll do just about anything," Granny said. "The truth be known, I bought the girl from them. Cost me some knives and blankets, a jug of coffin varnish, and a rifle, but it's worth it to have her safe."

"You gave a rifle to a hostile?" Jared's tone implied she had done a grievous wrong.

"An old Sharps," Granny said. "I only had four shells so it's not like Lame Bear will wipe out the white race."

Fargo was more interested in the other item she mentioned. "You sell whiskey? Where and how much?" He fished in his pocket for his money.

Granny grinned and said, "You remind me of my George. He never met a bottle he wouldn't suck down. A drummer sold me a case of whiskey a while back. I sell it to the Paiutes for ten dollars a bottle and most others for four dollars. But you can have one for two." She motioned. "I reckon it's all right for you to go in. Just don't wake up sweet little Mandy."

Fargo had never seen a trading post so tidy and clean. There wasn't a speck of dust anywhere. The floor was spotless. All the trade goods were neatly arranged in piles, stacks, or rows.

The whiskey bottles shared shelf space with bottles of rum, Scotch, and vodka. There were even a few bottles of wine.

Leaning the Henry against the counter, Fargo took a bottle down, opened it, and indulged in a long swig. A familiar burning sensation spread down his throat to the pit of his stomach. Smacking his lips, he grabbed the Henry and was near the door when there was a loud yelp and the patter of feet.

"Mr. Flint!" Mandy squealed. Throwing herself at his legs, she wrapped her arms tight and started crying, she was so happy.

Tucking the bottle under one arm, Fargo pried her loose and squatted. Her face was streaked with grime and the tracks of dry tears. Her nightshirt was dirty but otherwise she appeared to be fine. "Did they hurt you?"

Mandy shook her head. "Lame Bear said so long as I behaved nothing would happen to me."

"He speaks English?"

"A little." Mandy hugged him, her cheek on his shoulder. "He scares me, Mr. Flint. Scares me something awful."

"He's gone now," Fargo assured her.

"Lame Bear has a necklace made of teeth from all the white people he's killed. He hates us. He told me so himself. He's meaner than anyone I've ever met." Mandy shivered, and not because she was cold. "Granny gave him a lot of stuff so he would set me free. He wouldn't do it until she gave him a rifle. They argued and argued." Mandy drew back. "She's a nice lady. She fed me and tucked me in and said the rest of you would show up soon. And here you are." She glanced at the door. "Where's Ma?"

"I came on ahead." Picking her up, Fargo turned to the door.

"She'll be here soon, won't she?" the girl anxiously asked.

"Tomorrow or the next day," Fargo predicted. With her in one arm and his rifle and the bottle in the other, he awkwardly pried at the latch and pushed the door open with the toe of his boot.

Granny took one look, raised the Walker Colt, and thumbed back the hammer. "I thought I warned you not to wake her up."

9

For a few seconds Skye Fargo thought Grandma Barnes would squeeze the trigger. A steely glint came into her eyes and her jaw muscles twitched and her trigger finger started to tighten. Then she laughed and lowered the Walker Colt and carefully let down the hammer.

"Come here, child, and let Granny give you a hug!"

Fargo set Mandy down and she ran into the older woman's arms. Tossing off another swig of whiskey, he wiped his mouth with his sleeve.

"Yes, sir," Granny said, looking at him over Mandy's shoulder. "More and more like my George by the minute. He had the manners of a goat, too. But I did so love him despite his flaws." Holding Mandy at arm's length, she said, "Mr. Flint and Mr. Fox came to take you back. Or you can wait here if you would like until your mother and the wagon train arrive."

The suggestion irritated Fargo. Sarah must be half out of her mind with worry, and would want to see her daughter as soon as possible.

Mandy turned. "What do you think, Mr. Flint? Should I go with you or wait for my ma?"

"If you ask me, child," Jared butted in, "you're safer here than anywhere else. The Paiutes won't bother you. And you have a roof over your head and all the comforts of home."

"But my ma," Mandy said.

"Is hurrying to you even as we speak," Jared answered. "So why not wait here out of the heat and the dust?"

Fargo quickly said, "If she stays, you stay." He figured that Jared would rather be with his sister.

"Don't you trust her with me?" Granny took exception. "I would never let anyone harm a precious hair on her pretty head."

"Her mother would feel better knowing one of us was with her," Jared said, and straightened. "Very well, Mr. Flint. I'll remain here. But be sure to tell Cathy this wasn't my idea."

Granny cheerfully pinched Mandy's cheek. "You and I will have lots of fun. We can knit. We can play checkers. I have a deck of cards somewhere, and dominoes. All children your age love dominoes."

Mandy glanced at Fargo. "What do you think I should do?"

"It's your decision." Fargo did not want to appear too tenderhearted so he gruffly added, "Just make up your mind so I can be on my way. The faster I get back, the faster I can bring her to you."

"I'll stay, then, I guess," Mandy said, but she was not happy about it.

Fargo walked to the hitch rail and led the Ovaro toward the spring. A fence surrounded it, and the only way in was through a wide gate which was padlocked. "What the hell?" he grumbled.

"Did you think the water was free?" Granny had come up behind him without him noticing. For an older woman she was exceptionally light on her feet. "I charge for it just like I do everything else. Fifty cents for two-legged critters, a dollar for horses, cows, oxen, and mules."

"Trying to outdo Midas?"

Granny grinned. "Having money never hurt anyone. I was here first. I have the right to do as I want."

"The Paiutes were here first," Fargo corrected her. "Do you charge them too?"

"I'm not stupid, Mr. Flint. There are limits to how far Indians can be pushed. They get to drink and graze their ponies for free provided they behave themselves." Granny produced an iron key and slid it into the padlock. "They never use much though. Wagons trains are another matter. They drink until they're fit to burst, then fill up their water barrels with more. That doesn't count the water for their animals. To me it's only fair to have folks pay for the privilege."

Fargo let the Ovaro drink first. He was more interested in the tracks in the soft earth at the water's edge. Footprints of men, women, and children, and animals of all kinds, jumbled together like the pieces of a jigsaw.

"I don't suppose you're interested in a job?" Granny asked out of nowhere.

"I have one," Fargo said.

"Piloting is a lot of hard work and long hours," Granny mentioned. "Why go through all that when you don't have to?"

"What would I do?" Fargo did not see where she needed help.

"Whatever I want. There are always odd jobs to be done. Chinks in the walls to fill in. Sweep the floor. Carry heavy goods I can't manage on my own. That sort of stuff."

"I'll think about it," Fargo said, but he had no intention of giving her offer a second thought. Squatting, he dipped his hand in the spring and sipped from his palm. The water was deliciously cool. He scooped a second handful, and a third. "How much does my fifty cents buy me?"

"All day and all night. I'm not greedy." Granny stroked the Ovaro's neck. "Nice critter you have here. I haven't seen many quite like him. Would you consider selling?"

"Not while I'm still breathing." Fargo removed his hat and lowered it into the spring.

"You have a weakness for horses as well as children. Interesting."

"Who says?" Fargo upended the hat over his head and the water spilled down over his face and under his shirt in front and in back. For a while, at least, he would be wonderfully cool.

"Don't deny you're fond of the girl," Granny said. "I could see it on your face. You're not as tough as you make yourself out to be."

Fargo jammed his hat back on and rose. "Cross me," he told her, "and you'll find out." He paid her and forked leather. As he rode past the porch Mandy waved at him. He glanced back to be sure Granny Barnes could not see him, and waved. Then he applied his spurs.

Fargo had a lot to think about. He had established there was indeed a trading post and there might well be a trail over the Sierra Nevadas he had never heard of, but the big question still went unanswered: what had happened to the missing wagon trains?

Engrossed in thought, Fargo was only a hundred yards shy of the canyon mouth when his instincts flared. Once again a shadow flitted from boulder to boulder along the west rim, pacing him.

Pretending not to notice, Fargo held the pinto to a walk until he reached the end of the canyon. Then, abruptly reining the Ovaro, he headed up a steep slope as fast as the stallion could manage. Clods of dirt and rocks clattered out from under its driving hooves. Above him a face stared down in surprise. In a twinkling it was gone, its owner in flight.

Bending forward to distribute his weight more evenly, Fargo slapped his legs against the Ovaro's sides. The slope had become more treacherous and the stallion was fighting for purchase. Twenty more yards and they reached the top, and Fargo palmed his Colt.

The skulker was in full flight, weaving among the boulders with a speed and agility worthy of an antelope.

Fargo gave chase; whoever it was might pose a threat to Mandy. His quarry wore a baggy brown shirt and pants and a brown hat that blended into the terrain, but Fargo would be damned if he would lose sight of him. The stallion swiftly gained.

Suddenly the skulker looked back, the upper half of his face shrouded by the shadow of his hat brim, and bent at the waist so he was harder to spot. It did him no good. Bit by bit Fargo whittled the other's lead until he was only a few yards behind him. His quarry was winded and running slower.

Vaulting from the saddle, Fargo broke into a run. He was close enough to hear the rasp of the other's labored breaths and the *thap-thap-thap* of the other's shoes smacking the hard ground. Fargo poured on a last spurt of speed and slammed the Colt against the man's side.

Knocked off balance, the skulker careened against a boulder, cried out, and sprawled forward. His hat went flying.

Fargo cocked the Colt and pressed it against the back of the man's head. "Stay right where you are."

The man froze.

"Who are you and what are you up to?"

In a voice as melodious as music, the lurker replied, "Granny told me to hide until you were gone. We knew you were coming. She told me that you're the hombre who made buzzard bait of Raskum."

"I'll be damned." Gripping her by the shoulder, Fargo rolled her over. "You're female." She had sandy hair cropped short and a round face with hazel eyes. He guessed her age to be between twenty and twenty-five. "What's your name?"

"Melissa Barnes. I'm Granny's granddaughter." Melissa stared at the Colt and cringed. "You're not fixing to shoot me, are you?"

"Not unless you run off again," Fargo said dryly. Shoving the Colt into his holster, he hauled her to her feet.

Melissa had lost some of her fear. "Granny will be mad at me. I was supposed to lie low but I was curious. We don't get many visitors."

"You will once word of the Barnes Trail spreads," Fargo mentioned to see what she would say.

"Most likely," Melissa said, and smoothed her shirt. In doing so, she inadvertently accented the swell of her breasts and the flair of her hips. Under those baggy clothes was a sleek but voluptuous body.

Fargo tore his gaze from her chest to her face. "Tell your grandmother I didn't know who you were or I wouldn't have ridden you down."

"You must be kidding? She'll take a switch to my hide if she finds out. I won't say a thing if you don't."

"You have my word." Fargo turned to retrace his steps to the Ovaro. Sarah would be anxiously awaiting word of her daughter.

Melissa skipped to his side, "Will you take me down with you? On your horse, I mean?"

"To the trading post? I thought you didn't want your grandmother to know we've met?"

"Just to the mouth of the canyon," Melissa said. "I'll walk back from there." She scampered ahead and regarded the Ovaro with delight.

"He's beautiful, mister! I love horses. Granny does, too. But she won't let me have one of my own."

"Why not?" Fargo had never heard of someone her age being denied the right to ride.

"She thinks I'll get into too much trouble."

"Oh. The Paiutes," Fargo thought he understood.

"Lame Bear and his bunch?" Melissa giggled. "They don't dare lay a finger on me. Not if they know what's good for them. No, Granny is afraid I'll head off for Denver or San Francisco or some place like that to find me a man."

"Looking to get hitched, are you?" Fargo asked as he climbed on.

"Mercy me, no. Not for five or ten years yet, if then." An impish grin curled Melissa's lips. "I just like men, is all. Had this hankering ever since my—," she caught herself, then said, "ever since this fella did me one night in the woodshed about ten years ago."

Fargo lowered his arm. She gripped it with both hands and he swung her up behind him. Her breasts brushed his back as she leaned against him, her arms around his shoulders.

"My, you're a big one." Melissa squeezed his biceps. "And all these muscles! How about if you show them to me?"

"You're not one for beating around the bush."

"Life is too short to pussyfoot around," Melissa said. "I learned at an early age that if you want something in this world, you have to reach out and grab it while it's there to be had. Men included."

"Some other time," Fargo said.

"Why not now?" Melissa asked, rubbing her cheek across his back. "I promise to make it worth your while."

"I can't. I have to do a friend a favor."

Melissa straightened. "It has something to do with that girl Lame Bear brought, doesn't it? Oh well. You'll be back this way, I reckon, and I'll still be here."

The steep slope spread out below them and Fargo started down. He leaned back to make it easier on the Ovaro and in doing so pressed against Melissa, who did not seem to mind one bit.

"Tell me something, mister. Have you ever been to those places I mentioned?"

"Both, and many more," Fargo said.

"Are they all I've heard? Do the ladies wear elegant dresses and ride around in fancy carriages and go to the theater and balls and stuff like that?"

"Some do. Some work themselves to the bone and can barely afford a new dress once a year."

"That won't be me," Melissa confidently vowed. "I aim to live in grand style. Which city would you recommend? Out of all the ones you've been to?"

Fargo answered without hesitation, "New Orleans."

"Why?"

"There's a lot of old money. French and Spanish families who were there before it became part of the United States. There's a lot of new money, Americans who have struck it rich and want to live where their riches can buy them the best there is to be had. A pretty woman like you could go far."

"Pretty? Me?" Melissa removed her hat and fluffed at her hair. "I don't get told that nearly enough."

She was silent until they reached the bottom and Fargo twisted to lend her a hand climbing down. Clinging to him, she traced tiny circles in his palm. "Are you sure I can't persuade you to change your mind?"

Fargo thought of Sarah and reluctantly shook his head.

"Until we meet again, then, handsome. Don't let those pesky Paiutes get you." Tittering, Melissa pranced on up the canyon.

An interesting pair, Granny and her granddaughter, Fargo thought to himself as he trotted off. In more ways than one.

10

Fargo knew something was wrong the moment he saw the prairie schooners. There were eight, not nine, creaking and rattling their way toward the Blood Red mountains.

Peter Sloane saw him coming and brought the lead wagon to a halt. The rest followed suit. Sloane's wife averted her face, as if she were embarrassed. Sloane placed a hand on the rifle beside him on the seat and said, "So you're back. I was sincerely hoping we had seen the last of you. Where's young Jared?"

"Waiting at the Barnes Trading Post." Fargo looked down the line. "Whose wagon is missing? Did someone break a wheel and fall behind?"

"Nothing like that," Sloane said. "Sarah Yager refused to break camp this morning. I warned her that we would leave her if she didn't hitch her oxen and get ready to move out, but all she did was sit there crying."

"You *left* her?" Fury boiled up in Fargo like scalding hot water boiling up in a pot. "After what happened to her daughter?"

"That's why we had to keep going," Sloane tried to justify what he had done. "We're too easy to pick off out here on these damned flats. As leader, it's my responsibility to do what is best for the common good. I can't put everyone in peril because of one person."

"You damn coward," Fargo growled. "If anything has happened to her, you'll answer to me." He began to ride off but Mrs. Sloane thrust a hand at him.

"Wait! Please! What about Mandy? Did you find her?"

"She's safe at the trading post." Fargo got out of there before he pulled Peter Sloane from the seat and beat him senseless. As he passed the other wagons Cathy Fox and Jurgensen called out to him but he galloped on by. They were as much to blame as Sloane; they should have refused to abandon one of their own.

Fargo tried not to think of what the renegades would do if they found Sarah first. Lame Bear hadn't touched Mandy but Mandy was a child. A grown woman would not be so lucky.

It was hours before the white canvas hump appeared in the distance. Fargo's dread mounted when he saw the oxen a hundred yards from the schooner, their massive heads hung low. "Sarah?" he hollered when he was still a ways out but she didn't appear. Then he saw her, under the wagon at the rear. He slowed, his blood becoming ice, and yanked the Henry out. A quick scan of the alkali flats revealed no other riders. Dismounting, he crouched to peer underneath.

Sarah was on her back, her long hair half over her face. There was no blood, no wounds or marks. Fargo couldn't tell if she was breathing. "Sarah?" he said softly, and touched her leg.

Uttering a sharp cry, Sarah rose on her elbows and frantically scrambled backward. She blinked sleep from her eyes, stopped, and blurted, "It's only you! I dozed off and dreamed a Paiute was after me." She came scrambling toward him. "What about Mandy? Did you find her? Where is she?"

Fargo grasped her outstretched hand and pulled her out from under the wagon. "She's fine. I left her at the trading post."

Sarah gripped his shirt. "How could you? Why didn't you bring her? I've been half out of my mind!"

Fargo explained about Granny Barnes, and Jared, and the fact Melissa Barnes was there, as well.

"So there are women watching over her?" Sarah said, her panic fading. "Then my baby is really and truly all right?" Slumping against him, Sarah clung to his shoulders and burst into great racking sobs. She cried and cried until she had cried herself dry, and then she stepped back and wiped a sleeve across her face, saying, "Sorry. I've been holding a lot in. I couldn't eat, I couldn't hardly sleep."

"You're exhausted," Fargo said. "I'll hitch the team. You climb in the wagon and get some rest."

In half an hour they were under way, the Ovaro tied to the rear of the wagon. Now and then Fargo heard Sarah's snores above the rattle of the wheels and the dull shuffle of the plodding oxen. He was tired himself and could not resist an occasional yawn.

Fargo had a lot to ponder. Foremost was his next step once Sarah and Mandy were reunited. The army was counting on him to solve the disappearances, and once he took a job, he saw it through to the end.

Judging by the tracks, the other wagon trains had made it as far as the trading post. Whatever befell them took place after they left it. The army suspected the renegades were to blame, but Lame Bear and four warriors couldn't wipe out that many emigrants. Not without a lot of help. Maybe, Fargo speculated, there were more renegades involved than anyone suspected.

Another possibility was that disaster struck somewhere along the Barnes Trail. The emigrants might have run out of water, although the odds of that happening to all four wagon trains were high.

Fargo mentally swore at himself for being too hasty in getting rid of Swink, the one man who might have all the answers. He should have questioned him. Should have made Swink tell all he knew.

Hours dragged by. Nightfall found them still on the flats. Fargo pushed on another hour and a half to reach the foothills and halted the wagon between two hills, safe from searching eyes.

Sarah had slept the day away. Fargo let her go on sleeping as he gathered dry brush for a fire. A few eggs were left in the flour barrel. He also found the last of her bacon. Then he put on a pot of coffee to wash it all down.

The air was filled with the mouth-watering aroma of their meal when Fargo climbed onto the wagon. He had to shake her several times before she stirred.

"How long have I been out?" Sarah sleepily asked. Sitting up, she stretched, her breasts like ripe melons waiting to be plucked. "It's nighttime? Why didn't you get me up sooner?"

"You needed your rest." Fargo assisted her onto the seat and from there she swung lithely to the ground, her dress swirling about her thighs.

"You shouldn't have stopped. I want to reach the trading post as quickly as possible."

"Your horses are about played out," Fargo observed. "They need their rest, too. We'll reach the post by ten or so tomorrow morning."

"I can't wait that long," Sarah protested, angrily stamping a foot. "I can't bear to be separated from Mandy. She's all I have left in this world. All I live for."

"By now the wagon train is there. Your daughter will be fine." Fargo indicated a blanket he had bundled near the fire for her to sit on. Forking eggs and strips of sizzling bacon onto a plate, he gave it to her.

"You can cook in addition to everything else?" Sarah's sense of humor had returned. "You'll make some woman a find husband one day."

"I'm not settling down until I'm sixty," Fargo said. If then. He filled his own plate and ravenously dug in.

Sarah stared about them. "So it's just the two of us? Alone, all night long? What will we do with ourselves, Mr. Flint?" Her teeth shone white in the night.

"I'm sure we can think of something." Fargo filled her cup with hot black coffee, then filled his and swallowed half of it in two gulps. The jolt to his system was like being kicked by a mule. He ate with relish, had two more cups of coffee, and sat back, more than a little drowsy.

"I was so afraid," Sarah said. She had stopped eating and was picking at her eggs. "More afraid than I've ever been. If those Paiutes—" She stopped and put a hand to her forehead. "I don't know what I'd have done."

"It's over," Fargo said. Rising, he moved around the fire and sat next to her, deliberately rubbing his arm against hers. "You need to stop thinking about it and get on with your life."

"I'll never make a mistake like that again," Sarah declared. "I'll never leave her alone when I shouldn't."

Fargo slid an arm across her back. "Don't blame yourself. Blame Lame Bear. He's the one who will answer for stealing her."

"Are you going after him?"

"Once you're at the trading post." Fargo couldn't let the renegades go on harassing emigrants. "It will be days before the wagon train moves on." More than enough time for him to track the Paiutes down.

Sarah placed her hand on his. "You're taking it on yourself on our account?"

"Something has to be done," Fargo said. Now, while Lame Bear's band was still in the vicinity.

"Sloane can't figure you out," Sarah mentioned. "He and some of the others think you're a ruthless killer. I know better. There's more to you than you let on. A part of you that you're hiding."

"There's more to everyone," Fargo blunted her sally. "I'm helping you because I like you. It's that simple."

"I'm flattered, but I'm not stupid. I'll take what I can get, and when we part company, I won't have any regrets but one." Sarah's fingers tightened. "And we will part ways, won't we?"

Fargo nodded.

"I'm sorry to hear that. But I thank you for being honest with me." Sarah took her plate from her lap and placed it on the ground. "It doesn't change anything, though. I can't help how I feel." She pressed closer and glued her mouth to his in a long, languid, delectable kiss.

The night stood still. To the northwest a coyote raised its plaintive cry. To the southeast a mountain lion screamed.

Fargo could taste the eggs and bacon on her tongue. He ran a hand through her silken black hair down to the small of her back and around her hip to her thighs. She opened them to admit his questing fingers and he caressed her from her knees to her inner thigh.

"Mmmmmmmm," Sarah moaned. One of her hands imitated his. At the top of each caress she would cup his manhood.

A constriction formed in Fargo's throat. The hills receded into a haze. His world consisted of her and him and the sensations she sent rippling through his body. He tingled from toe to head.

Sarah whispered in his ears, "The whole time we've been eating I've been thinking about the other night. Remembering your hands on me. Remembering how it felt to have you inside me." She licked his earlobe.

"I want you inside me again. I want to forget what I've been through. Forget the horror."

Fargo silenced her with a kiss. He lowered his other hand and massaged and kneaded her legs. She spread them wider, her dress hiking to the middle of her thigh. Sliding his right hand up and under, he soon had his middle finger where he wanted it. She was wet for him, wet with desire and need. A tiny mew issued from her throat and her nails bit into his thigh.

Fargo shifted to accommodate the growing bulge in his pants. Sarah pulled him toward the ground but he broke their kiss and said, "Let me fetch a blanket."

"We don't need one." Her fingers pried at his gun belt and then at his pants and within moments Fargo felt air on his manhood. Her fingers were next. Enfolding him, she stroked up and down.

The walnut in Fargo's throat became an apple. He licked and kissed her neck until she wriggled and sighed and tried to shove him inside of her.

"Let me," Fargo said. He slowly rubbed his member up and down her womanhood, heightening her anticipation.

"Oh, yesssss," Sarah whispered. "I want you. I want you so much."

Inch by slow inch, Fargo slid himself into her. When he was all the way in he held himself motionless.

Not Sarah. She moved under him, her breasts grinding into his chest, her hips grinding into his. Another moan started and did not stop. It went on and on, rising in volume as she grew more and more aflame with the heat of passion.

On a nearby hill a warbler gave voice to its distinctive cry.

Slowly rocking on his knees, Fargo nibbled an ear, kissed her forehead and her cheek.

"You feel so good," Sarah husked. "Do you know that?"

Fargo gripped her hips for better leverage. The ground hurt his knees but he didn't care. He had a cramp in his left leg but he didn't care. His pants had bunched up low on his legs and were uncomfortable as hell but he didn't care. He thrust harder but not as hard as he could, not yet, not until they reached the summit.

The same bird twittered again.

Sarah's hands entwined in his hair and his hat fell off. A handful in each hand, she yanked so hard he thought his hair would come out by the roots. "Don't stop! Please don't stop!"

The breeze had picked up and was cooling the sweat on Fargo's skin. He moved faster, instinct taking over. His mind drifted on a sea of sensation. He gave no thought to the Paiutes or the army or the missing wagon trains or anything or anyone other than the throbbing deep in his core.

"Oh, Flint!" Sarah said. "I'm there!" Her release was a wild paroxysm of thrashing and moaning and gushing.

Fargo had to hold on to keep from being bucked off. She drenched him, and drenched him again, her hips a blur, her inner walls contracting and rippling and squeezing. He lasted half a minute more. Then there was no plugging the dyke. The hills and the stars turned topsy-turvy. His breath caught in his throat. He impaled her over and over until, totally spent, he collapsed on top of her, his head cushioned by her heaving breasts.

Gradually they stopped panting and their slick bodies stilled.

Sarah nipped his cheek, then sighed contentedly. "I needed that more than you can possibly imagine. I'm not mad anymore that you left Mandy at the trading post. It was the right thing to do."

Once more the warbler sounded, closer now. But

this time the warble came from the north, not the south, as the other cries had. An answer came from the west, then an echo from the east.

Only then did Fargo realize they were not birds at all.

11

Skye Fargo had been caught with his pants down before and it was not an experience he cared to repeat. Quickly rolling onto his shoulder, he pulled them up and buckled on his gun belt. Reclaiming his hat, he drew his Colt and peered intently into the darkness, seeking the sources of the birdlike cries.

The Ovaro, Fargo now noticed, was facing the hill to the west in an attitude of alert watchfulness.

"What is it?" Sarah whispered. She had slid to one side and was pulling herself together. "What's out there?"

"I'm not sure yet." Taking hold of her wrist, Fargo skirted the fire, snatched up the Henry, and shoved it at her. He would not need it. At night, at close range, a pistol was just as effective. Backpedaling into the dark, he crouched. "Get under your wagon."

Sarah obeyed without argument. Crawling behind the front wheel, she poked the Henry between the spokes.

Fargo crept to the south a dozen yards, and hunkered. To his right a twig snapped, to his left a rock was dislodged and rolled down the slope. Whoever was out there was either overconfident or possessed all the stealth of a tree stump. Which made him doubt it was the Paiutes.

The ratchet of a cartridge being fed into a chamber warned Fargo another bushwhacker was somewhere in front of him. He looked for a moving shadow, for a target of any kind, but saw none.

Then, out of the brush to the north of the prairie schooner came a shout. "You there! Throw down your guns and come out where we can see you with your hands in the air!"

Fargo saw Sarah poke her head out. She had lost sight of him and was unsure what to do. He hoped she had the presence of mind to stay where she was.

"Didn't you hear me?" the man bellowed. "We have you surrounded! Do as we say, and do it now!"

On the hill to the west someone cackled. A rifle spanged, the slug kicking up dirt near the fire. "That's just a warning!" the shooter warned.

Fargo had located two of them but he still could not see anyone. The soft crunch of a stealthy footstep remedied that. A vague shape was coming down the hill to the east in short, jerky steps. Fargo took aim but didn't shoot. He wanted the man closer so he couldn't miss.

A shout from Sarah, though, caused the man to freeze. "Who are you? What do you want?"

"We're federal law officers," replied the one to the north. "Do as we say and no one will be hurt."

It was a trick. Fargo hoped to God Sarah didn't believe him. The territory didn't have duly appointed federal officers yet.

"If you're law officers," Sarah responded, "why are you sneaking up on us? Why didn't you come right up to our fire?"

"And be shot in our tracks? Throw your guns down and we'll come out in the open, but not before."

"A true law officer would not be afraid to show himself," Sarah argued.

The man had an answer for everything. "If you have

nothing to hide, why did the man you're with disappear? Where is he?" His tone hardened. "For the last time, lady. Step out where we can see you. Both of you. We don't want to hurt you but we will if you force us."

Again Sarah looked around for Fargo. He dared not say anything, dared not wave to attract her attention, not with the others so close.

"We won't wait forever," the alleged lawman threatened.

"A real marshal would never shoot a woman," Sarah held her own. "If you're who you say you are, go away and come back in the morning. We'll still be here."

Another pebble rattled down the east hill. The shape Fargo had spotted was crossing an open space. A rifle glinted dully in the gloom.

On the west hill the rifleman who had fired was also in motion, angling toward the wagon, and Sarah.

That left the gunman to the south. Fargo thought the man was farther away than he was, for suddenly a dark form loomed against the stars and trained a rifle on the wheel Sarah was crouched behind. This one was short. Five feet tall, if that, and wore a cowhide vest and a low-crowned hat.

"Drop it," Fargo whispered.

The short gunman mimicked mesquite but he didn't let go of his rifle. Moonlight played over his pudgy face as his beady eyes shifted back and forth. "There you are," he grunted. "You must be part Apache."

Fargo held the Colt so the man could plainly see it. "I won't tell you twice."

"Go ahead and shoot. I swear I'll put a bullet into your woman friend before I go down," the short man said, none too quietly. "You're the one who had better drop his hardware if you know what's good for you."

The man on the east slope heard and swung toward them. The shooter on the west hill checked his descent.

"What will it be, mister?" the short one demanded.

Fargo shot him. Not in the head or the heart but high in the right shoulder. The impact spun the short gunman completely around. His rifle thudded to the ground and the man crumpled.

Almost instantly the shooter on the west hill cut loose, firing twice as rapidly as he could work the lever.

Fargo dived flat as leaden hornets buzzed by.

"Don't shoot, damn you, Thorn!" the short one wailed, holding his shoulder. "You'll hit me!"

That did not stop the man on the west hill. He fired twice more and one of the rounds drilled into the earth inches from Fargo's face.

"Stop shooting!" the short gunman screeched. "Dix, make him stop!"

Fargo snapped off a shot at the man to the west, twisted, and snapped off another at the gunman to the east. Both melted into the shadows. He glanced at the prairie schooner just as Sarah started to rise from under it. "Stay down!" he bellowed, and had to hug the ground as rifles blasted on both sides and dirt stung his cheeks and neck.

"Thorn! Preston!" the man to the north yelled. "That's enough! Do you hear me?"

The men on the hills obeyed.

The short one was gritting his teeth and quaking in agony, an inky stain spreading across his cowhide vest.

Crawling over, Fargo gouged the Colt against the gunman's temple and clamped his other hand on the back of the man's neck. "What's your name?"

"Everyone calls me Shorty," the man bleated.

"Do you want to live?"

"*Now* you ask? After you've put lead in me?" Shorty groaned as if to demonstrate how much pain he was in.

"I can always finish the job," Fargo said. "Or would you rather do as I say and live?" When Shorty didn't answer, he cocked the Colt.

"All right, all right. Don't get your dander up. For now you're holding the high card."

"Tell your friends to throw down their rifles and step into the light," Fargo directed.

Shorty sneered through his agony. "Wishful thinking. Dixon is too smart. And Thorn won't shed his guns for anyone."

"Let's find out." Fargo took Shorty's revolver and wedged it under his own belt, then rose, hauling Shorty with him, and propelled Shorty to the edge of the firelight. "Have a look!" he shouted. "I've got a gun to his head! Step out where I can see you!"

"Not a chance!" hollered the rifleman on the west hill.

"I told you Thorn wouldn't agree," Shorty said nervously.

The man to the north was more reasonable. "Don't do anything drastic. You let him go, and I give you my word we'll leave you in peace."

"That's Dix," Shorty said. "You can trust him. He never breaks his word once he gives it."

Fargo wouldn't trust any of them as far as he could throw the prairie schooner. "The three of you get on your horses and ride. When you're a ways off, each of you fire a shot into the air, one right after the other. Only then does Shorty go free."

Thorn swore lustily, then shouted, "I don't back down for any man! It's Shorty's own fault for being stupid enough to be caught!"

"You'll do as I tell you!" Dixon commanded. "Preston, you and Thorn meet me at the horses. Shorty, don't worry. I'm not about to let anything happen to you."

In a few moments boots drummed to the north and east but Thorn lingered, his rifle to his shoulder. Then he made a savage gesture, wheeled, and ran off up over the hill.

"He's always been the mean one," Shorty commented.

"You're not lawmen," Fargo stated the obvious. "So you must be outlaws out to rob us."

Shorty started to laugh but grunted and clutched his shoulder. "Shows how much you know, mister. This was a social visit, believe it or not."

"I don't," Fargo said. Four armed men sneaking up on a camp in the dead of night were not up to any good.

"Makes no never mind to me, Flint. We were only doing what we were told. But you putting lead into me changes things. It wasn't very nice."

Fargo almost swung Shorty around to look him in the face and see if he was serious. "How is it you know my name?"

"A little bird told me," Shorty said.

The only ones who knew Fargo was calling himself Flint were Colonel McCormack and a few soldiers, the emigrants with Sloane's party, and the old woman and her granddaughter at the trading post. Fargo was tempted to ask about the missing wagon trains but if he did Shorty might suspect the real reason he was there.

"There's a lot more going on here than you reckon," Shorty bragged. "You're lucky you didn't kill me or the rest would track you to the ends of the earth and put windows in your noggin."

"The rest?" Fargo said, but Shorty didn't take the bait.

Sarah had slid from under the wagon and was coming toward them. She prudently skirted the fire. "Who are these men? What did they want?"

Shorty's slit of a mouth curled in a grin. "What do you think we'd want with a gal as pretty as you? I hope I get to go first when we draw straws."

Fargo gripped Shorty by his wounded shoulder, and squeezed.

Yelping, Shorty nearly folded at the knees. "Damn you! That was uncalled for. What I want to do isn't any different from what you were doing ten minutes ago."

"You saw us?" Sarah was aghast.

"I didn't see enough, I'm sorry to say," Shorty taunted her. "But I'd love to have those legs of yours wrapped around me."

The night rumbled to the drum of hooves. Fargo established they were heading west, and poked Shorty with his Colt. "Where did the four of you come from? What's out here that would interest men like you?"

"You're a regular bundle of questions," Shorty replied. "But I'm not the one to answer them. I follow orders like all the rest."

"Whose orders?"

Shorty shook his head. "Gouge out my eyes and I won't say. You're big and tough as sin, but I know someone a lot meaner. Someone who thinks nothing of doing things to people that would curdle your blood. Someone who once gutted a baby for the fun of it."

"No!" Sarah exclaimed.

"I've seen women skinned alive," Shorty crowed. "Seen men tied upside down to trees and fires started under them so their brains bake. Seen an old woman made to swallow broken glass." Shorty locked eyes with Fargo. "So do your worst, Flint. It can't be half as bad as what they would do."

"Who did all those things?" Fargo asked. "You and your friends?"

"Wouldn't you like to know?" Shorty was growing smug. "Let's just say we're the curliest wolves you're ever likely to meet."

"Then how is it the old woman at the trading post is still alive?"

Shorty snickered. "Are you kidding? She's meaner than all of us combined, her with that old Walker Colt." He laughed, then said, "Why would we kill Granny? Where's the sense in riding all the way to Fort Bridger or Fort Hall for supplies when we can get all we need from her?"

As Fargo recollected, that was the same reason Granny Barnes gave for the Paiutes leaving her alone. But she was living on a razor's edge. Outlaws and renegades were notoriously unreliable, and notoriously vicious.

Shorty touched his wound, and grimaced. "It's not hurting nearly as much. The bullet went clean through or I'd be bleeding a lot more."

"You're taking it awful calmly," Sarah said.

"Hell, it's not as if I haven't been shot before. This makes the fourth, no, the fifth time. Once in each leg and once in my arm and another time in my backside. I'm unlucky that way. The others always tease me about it."

Fargo was listening for hooves or footfalls; he wouldn't put it past the outlaws to circle back. "What are your plans for the wagon train?"

"What makes you think we have any? The four of us aren't hankering to be shot to pieces."

"Which one of you runs things?" Fargo probed, but before Shorty could answer, gunfire crackled a quarter of a mile away.

"They've held up their end," Shorty said. "Now I expect you to hold up yours." He took a step west-

95

ward, then stopped and held out his left hand. "My pistol, if you please?"

Fargo emptied the cylinder, then tossed it to him. "We'll meet again."

"You can count on it, mister."

They watched until Shorty was lost to view, and Sarah remarked, "I wonder what that was all about?"

"We'll find out soon enough," was Fargo's hunch.

12

The emigrants had found paradise. Their prairie schooners were parked in a long row in the shade of trees near the trading post. Their horses had been let loose to graze. The children played tag or hide and seek. Many of the men were at ease on the porch, many of the women were inside admiring the trade goods.

Mandy came bounding like a young rabbit. Sarah was off the wagon before Fargo brought it to a complete stop, and mother and daughter embraced and clung to one another, weeping.

As Fargo climbed down, Sarah glanced at him and mouthed the words, "Thank you." He touched his hat brim, then untied the Ovaro from the back of the prairie schooner and brought it to the hitch rail.

"The two of you made it," Peter Sloane said, not sounding particularly pleased. He was leaning against a porch post and puffing on a cigar. "All your worry was for nothing, eh?"

"For nothing," Fargo said. Stepping onto the porch, he gripped Sloane by the shirt, spun him completely around, and punched him on the jaw. Sloane teetered on the edge of the porch a moment, then down he went, dazed but not severely hurt.

Everyone else froze.

Fargo stepped off the porch and reached Sloane just

as Sloane rose onto his hands and knees. "That was for deserting Mrs. Yager." Snapping Sloane erect, he delivered a blow to the gut. "That was for making them ride last all the time." Fargo leaned down, slapped Sloane's hands away, and hauled Sloane to his feet a second time. "And this is for all the trouble you've given me."

His arms pinwheeling, Peter Sloane landed hard on his back. Like an upended turtle he lay glaring, and spitting blood. "I didn't deserve that!"

"Yes, you did," Fargo said. "That and a lot worse. We were almost killed, thanks to you."

"Me?" Sloane spit more blood and pushed to his feet. "Whatever befell you out there, you brought it on yourselves."

"Always making excuses," Fargo said. "Have you ever owned up to your mistakes once your whole life?"

"If you didn't have that pistol," Sloane snarled, "I would thrash you within an inch of your miserable life."

"Oh?" Unbuckling his gun belt, Fargo gave it to Jurgensen. Sloane instantly waded into him while his back was turned. They weren't the precise blows of a professional boxer but they were backed by sinew and muscle that had pushed plows for years. Whatever else he might be, Sloane was no weakling. His punches hurt.

Circling, Fargo blocked and slipped swing after swing. He landed a few solid hits whenever an opening presented itself.

"Stop them!" someone cried.

"Not on your life!" Nickelby said. "They've been leading up to this since they met. It's high time they settled it."

Sloane was determined to, that was for sure. Adopting a stance like Fargo's, he began throwing his fists where they would do the most damage: at Fargo's cheeks, at Fargo's mouth and jaw, at Fargo's ribs.

Once he tried to knee Fargo in the groin but Fargo sprang back and countered with a right cross that rocked Sloane onto his boot heels.

Mrs. Sloane tried to intervene by stepping between them. "Peter, you cease this nonsense this instant!"

"Out of my way, woman!" Sloane roared, and shoved her so that she stumbled and nearly fell. "This is between the two of us!"

Fargo feinted, and when Sloane raised an arm to block, he slipped in a left jab that bent Sloane in half. "That one was for your wife."

The farmer was livid. "I'm going to kill you with my bare hands! Do you hear me? My bare hands!"

"Not today. Not ever."

"We'll see about that." Sloane came in fast and furious, rage and frustration making him reckless. He didn't bother with body blows. He went for the face and the throat.

Fargo blocked, spun, blocked again. A fist scraped his cheek. He flicked one past Sloane's guard to crash against Sloane's jaw but the farmer stayed on his feet and kept coming. A woman yelled something, Mrs. Sloane maybe, but whatever she yelled was lost in the whirl of combat.

Sloane's cheek was split and his lips were bloody and puffy and he had a nasty welt over one eye. Huffing and husking, he stormed at Fargo yet again, his thick arms cracking like whips.

A left hook glanced off Fargo's jaw and for a few seconds the world spun. Then Peter Sloane's head filled his vision and he delivered an uppercut that started at his knees and ended a foot in the air above Sloane's head. He heard a *thud* and looked down and the farmer was sprawled at his feet, unconscious to the world.

Breathing deeply, Fargo slowly lowered his arms and stepped back. Sloane had put up more of a fight than he thought. He moved toward the porch, his ribs aching with every step. The emigrants moved out of his way. Jurgensen gave him the gun belt and he strapped it on and went inside and over to the liquor shelf. He had finished the first bottle before he lit out after the wagon train. Another was in order. Opening it, he upended it and chugged.

"Yes, sir. You'll drink yourself into an early grave just like my George." Granny Barnes was in the doorway, her smile warm and friendly. She wore a yellow bonnet and a wide leather belt decorated with blue and red flowers. Tucked under it was the big Walker Colt. "That will be four dollars."

"I thought mine only cost two?" Fargo said, reaching into his pocket.

"I should charge you double for the ruckus you just caused," Granny said sternly. "What got into you, tearing into him like that?"

"Jackasses always rub me the wrong way." Fargo flipped the money to her and she deftly caught it. "It's a failing of mine."

Granny chuckled. "I have a few failings myself but you couldn't pry them out of me with a metal bar." Walking behind the counter, she rummaged on a low shelf and produced a large tin box. From under the top of her dress she drew a necklace. A key hung from the end of it. She inserted the key into the lock on the box and opened the lid. Inside were stacks of bills and a collection of coins to which she added the ones he just gave her.

"Aren't you worried someone will steal that?" Fargo idly asked.

"Over my dead body." Granny closed the box and locked it and placed it under the counter again.

Fargo's lower lip was stinging from where Sloane had split it. He winced as he swallowed, then asked, "Where did Jared Fox get to?"

"Off with my granddaughter, I suppose," Granny said. "The two of them hit it off. But then, she hits it off with just about any male who happens by."

"Oh?" Fargo said, feigning innocence.

"That's right. You haven't met her yet, have you? Mr. Fox is fortunate she met him first or she wouldn't give him the time of day. She's partial to big, handsome scoundrels like you."

Fargo walked to the door. Sloane was still on the ground being tended by his wife and two other women. The men had moved off the porch and were over by the wagons, talking.

"Some of those pilgrims sure don't like you much, judging by the looks they're giving you," Granny said at his elbow.

Fargo downed more whiskey.

"I've overheard a few of them say they can't figure you out," Granny mentioned. "A walking contradiction, one called you."

"I care what they think," Fargo said sarcastically.

"I'm a mite puzzled myself, Mr. Flint. You forced yourself on them. You shot Raskum. You went after the girl. You helped the mother. Now you beat the stuffing out of their leader." Granny paused. "Are you for them or against them?"

"I'm for me." Fargo strode out into the sunlight and over to the hitch rail. Leading the pinto by the reins, he took it around the building to the spring. The gate hung open. He thought he was shed of Granny Barnes but she had followed him.

"Mr. Sloane paid fifty dollars to have the run of the spring for his whole party as long as they're here." Granny smirked. "He specifically said that does not include you."

Fargo paid her. While the Ovaro drank, he plopped down in the grass, his hands behind his head. "Are you still here?"

"Just tell me if I'm annoying you," Granny said.

"You're annoying me." Fargo had to keep up his act for as long as it took, no matter who it hurt.

"Forthright as can be." Granny winked. "I like that in a man. I wish my George had your gumption."

"I thought we were a lot alike."

"Only when it comes to bug juice," Granny said. "He had no more backbone than a bowl of soup. He could never make up his mind, for one thing. For another, he was too soft. He'd let people drink our water for free if it were up to him. Or charge half what I do for our goods." She fingered her bonnet. "He'd let people walk right over him, the simpleton."

"I've known men like that," Fargo said, but Granny did not appear to be listening.

"For the life of me, I can't remember why I married him. No woman wants a husband weaker than she is. No woman wants a man who won't stand up for himself. I wore the pants in our family. I was the one who did what had to be done."

Fargo motioned at the trading post. "You've done fine."

"You would think so, wouldn't you?" Granny said. "But I can't help wanting more. I've always been that way. I'm never satisfied. I suspect when I die, they'll carve that on my headstone."

A couple came strolling out of the trees hand in hand. Fargo had to smile when he saw it was Jared and Melissa. Jared was wearing his best Sunday-go-to-meeting clothes, Melissa a fetching dress.

Granny followed his gaze. "She's doing it again. Throwing herself at him. The boy is smitten but to her it's just another dalliance. She'll drop him like a hot ember if someone else takes her interest." Granny waggled a finger at him. "It could be you, Mr. Flint."

"I'm not interested."

"Don't let her boyish looks fool you. I hate to say

this about my own kin, but from what others say, she's a regular wildcat under the sheets."

Jared and Melissa stopped and kissed.

"Look at that!" Granny rasped. "Always flaunting herself when she shouldn't. Kindly excuse me, Mr. Flint." She bustled out of the gate and bore down on the pair like an irate she-bear.

Fargo gazed at the pond and saw the reflection of someone coming up behind him. "I hear your brother is in love."

Cathy Fox had on a clean sky-blue dress and had tied her blond hair back with a bright blue ribbon. Sashaying around in front of him, she frowned at her sibling. "Is that what they call it these days?"

"You don't approve?"

"Melissa Barnes has the morals of a minx. Last night she did everything but rip his clothes off in front of everyone. Now he's talking about proposing to her and taking her with us. Can you imagine?"

Fargo offered the whiskey bottle, not really expecting her to accept, but she did. Cathy took a tentative sip, scrunched up her face, and handed it back.

"How anyone can drink something that tastes like horse urine is beyond me."

"Tasted a lot of piss, have you?" Fargo asked, and moved his leg when she aimed a playful kick.

Cathy smacked her lips in distaste. "Milk, water, and an occasional glass of wine suit me just fine." She sank to the grass beside him. "At last we are alone, and I've so wanted to talk to you."

"About what?"

Granny and Melissa were heatedly arguing in low voices. The object of their dispute, poor Jared, was nervously squirming like a worm on a hook.

"Us," Cathy said.

Fargo looked at her in surprise. She was as different from Sarah as day from night: cornstalk hair instead of raven tresses, a pale complexion instead of bronzed skin, thinner lips but a larger bosom, and legs that went on forever. "Did I miss something somewhere?"

"I suspect you never miss a thing," Cathy flattered him.

"Then where did this 'us' come from?"

"I like you, Flint. I like you a lot, and I would like to get to know you better. Yes, you're partial to Sarah, but that doesn't mean we can't be," she grinned seductively, "friendly."

Fargo was puzzled. She hadn't spoken three words to him since he went off after Mandy, and now here she was, doing exactly what she accused Melissa Barnes of doing. He remembered Granny saying someone had accused *him* of being a walking contradiction? Hell, he reflected, women had him beat all hollow.

"You intrigue me." A pink tinge crept into Cathy's cheeks. "I haven't forgotten your brazen comment the other day about seeing me without my clothes. No one has ever talked to me like that."

"Some women would slap my face."

"I should, were I as prim and proper as my brother expects me to be. But I was raised on a farm with cows and horses and chickens and hogs." Cathy shrugged. "Once you've seen a stallion with a mare, well, let's just say I'm not as shy about some things as I used to be." She placed her hand on his knee. "If I'm being too forward, say so and I'll go."

"Move your hand higher and ask me again."

Cathy laughed. Her pink tinge became red. "It's nice to know I haven't made a fool of myself. I was afraid you would say you weren't interested."

Fargo thought of all the women he had known, all the lovelies he had been intimate with. "That will be the day."

13

After their long, arduous ordeal, the emigrants were in need of some fun and frolic. Peter Sloane, his face black and blue and swollen, called everyone together prior to the supper hour and announced, "As tonight is our last night here, I propose that Jurgensen break out his fiddle after we eat and we have us a shindig."

"A dance!" Mrs. Nickelby squealed. "I do so love to dance!"

"All you ladies can put on your best dresses," Sloane said. "The men will spruce up, and we'll celebrate until the wee hours." He glanced toward the porch where Granny was knitting in her rocking chair and Melissa was leaning against a post. "Granny, we hope you and your granddaughter will honor us by taking part."

Fargo noticed that Sloane did not look his way. He was seated at the far end of the porch, his whiskey bottle half empty. It had no more effect on him than a glass of water would but he pretended it did. When he stood, he swayed and gripped a post for support. He walked unsteadily around the corner to where he had picketed the Ovaro, close to the building. Capping the bottle, he shoved it into a saddlebag, then went to the spring. Kneeling, he removed his hat and splashed water on his face. Footsteps approached, and he rose thinking it would be Sarah or Cathy, but it was neither.

"I swear you're avoiding me," Melissa Barnes said. "You didn't even come say hello when you got back."

"You were busy with Jared."

"It's not like he's my husband or anything," Melissa groused. "I'm free to talk to any man I want."

"Don't you like him?"

"He's boring as hell but he helped pass the time while you were gone." Melissa ran a finger down the front of his buckskin shirt. "It's you I've cottoned to."

"Is that why you were holding Jared's hands and massaging his lips with yours?" Fargo brought up.

"Oh, pshaw. I let him in my pants and now he thinks he's in love. He's even hinted he might ask for my hand in marriage. Can you believe it?" Melissa laughed derisively. "Men are such simpletons. It's easy as sin for a woman to wrap them around her little finger."

"And you love to do the wrapping," Fargo said. He started toward the gate but she snagged his sleeve.

"What's your hurry, big man? Everyone else is around front. There's just the two of us, and the woods aren't far off."

Fargo thought of what he said to Cathy Fox earlier, and grinned. "No thanks. I'm not interested."

"You don't want me?" Amazement gave way to anger and Melissa balled her fists. "I can't believe you are turning me down!"

"That makes two of us," Fargo said. But it would crush Jared if Jared found out, and he would not put it past Melissa to rub Jared's nose in it.

"What's the matter? Maybe my hair doesn't shine like the sun like his sister's does, and maybe I'm not as pretty as that Yager woman, but I've never had any complaints."

"That makes two of us," Fargo repeated. Again he tried to walk off but she dug her fingers into his arm.

"I take this as an insult."

Fargo pried her fingers off and pushed her hand away. "Take it any way you want." He thought that would be the end of it but she stepped in front of him and slapped him across the face. His hand was in motion before hers stopped, the *crack* of his palm on her cheek like the crack of a bullwhip.

Melissa staggered back. Stupefied, she raised her hand to the hand print on her cheek. Her anger was multiplied by ten. Snarling, she threw herself at him, her fingernails hooked to rake and claw. She slashed at his eyes, trying to blind him, raging, "You stinking son of a bitch!"

Catching hold of her wrists, Fargo held on as she thrashed and tugged. When she realized she couldn't break free, she kicked at his shins and his knees but he sidestepped or deflected most of them.

Suddenly Melissa stood stock still and raged, "I'll castrate you for this! Do you hear me? So help me God!"

Fargo bunched his shoulders to shove her to the ground but just then Jared Fox came running along the fence and through the gate. "What's going on here, Flint? Why are you manhandling her?"

"It's nothing," Fargo said. "A little disagreement." He let go.

A sly look came over Melissa. She ran to Jared and threw her arms around his neck. "He's lying, darling! He tried to have his way with me and I wouldn't let him so he hit me."

"That's not what happened," Fargo said, but Jared had already launched himself at him.

"How dare you!"

A fist whisked at Fargo's face but he easily blocked

it and grabbed Jared's arm. Spinning him around, Fargo swept his leg against Jared's ankles, dumping Jared onto his backside. Melissa swore and came at him again with her nails flashing. Fargo tripped her, too, so that she sprawled beside her misguided lover. "Don't get up," he warned them.

Melissa glared at Jared. "Are you just going to sit there? If you really and truly care for me, you wouldn't let him treat me like this."

"Pay her no mind," Fargo said. But he was wasting his breath. Men in love often did foolish things and Jared was no exception. The young farmer sprang up and lunged, and Fargo resorted to an uppercut.

Jared landed on his back and didn't move except for the fluttering of his eyelids.

"Never ask a boy to do a woman's job," Melissa said in disgust.

Fargo had put up with as much as he was going to. He rarely struck women but he was willing to make an exception in her case. So when she flung herself at him like a berserk banshee, he clipped her on the jaw. She folded like so much wet paper, right on top of Jared. He left them there and was almost to the Ovaro when Granny stepped from the shadows.

"You don't take any guff, do you, Mr. Flint?"

"Your granddaughter brought it on herself." Fargo wondered if she had been spying on them the whole time.

"She'll be furious when she comes around," Granny said, and grinned. "But goodness gracious, that was glorious! I would pay to see you hit her again. She's had it coming for a long time. Her with her airs and her men. If I were ten years younger, I'd beat her every day until her hide couldn't hold shucks."

Fargo bent and took his saddle blanket and threw it over the stallion's broad back, and smoothed it.

"Going somewhere?" Granny asked.

"For a little ride," was all Fargo would say.

"Don't leave on my granddaughter's account. You'll miss the merriment. I'm supplying free jugs for the men and cider for the ladies."

Fargo slung his saddle over the stallion and set to work on the cinch. "I won't be gone long."

"There's not much to see hereabouts," Granny mentioned. "Unless you count rocks and lizards. Why not stay and let your hair down with the rest?"

"The ride will clear my head," Fargo said, although his head did not need clearing. He had a purpose but it was not for her to know.

"You sure are a stubborn cuss. What if you run into the Paiute? Or those four men Sarah mentioned? The ones who jumped you last night?"

Fargo was hoping to. "I'll keep my eyes skinned. But they're most likely long gone by now." He slipped the Ovaro's bridle on and was reaching for the saddle horn when Granny tried one last time.

"Sarah will be disappointed. So will that blond gal who has been making cow eyes at you."

The saddle creaked as Fargo mounted and slipped his other boot in the stirrup. He clucked to the pinto and headed down the canyon. Some of the emigrants stopped what they were doing to stare. He glanced back as he went around the bend, and Granny was still watching. He cantered to the end of the canyon.

It would be dark in an hour. Fargo did not have a lot of time. Wagon ruts pointed southwest but he was not interested in them at the moment. He circled to the south.

Granny had told him there was only one way in and out of the canyon, but Fargo had reason to suspect otherwise. It had to do with the tracks around the spring. As the only water to be had, it drew every wild animal for miles around. Fargo had seen the prints of a bobcat, a fox and raccoons, and deer, to mention just a few. There had to be a game trail somewhere, and he hadn't gone half a mile when he found it. Worn by countless paws and hoofs, it wound toward the top of the canyon.

Drawing rein, Fargo slid the Henry out, and climbed. It was much too steep for the Ovaro. At several points he had to use his free arm for leverage. Midway to the top he stopped to scour the countryside for signs of life but saw none.

At the top Fargo had a hawk's-eye view of the entire canyon. Jared and Melissa were out front of the trading post, mingling with the other emigrants. Cooking pots had been hung over fires and the women were making supper. The men were loafing, the children playing. He did not see Granny.

The game trail wound down the other side toward the spring but Fargo did not take it. He had seen enough to know that a rider could not use it. Returning to the Ovaro, he continued south until he came to a narrow break in the canyon wall. He almost went on by. Then he saw the horse tracks leading into it.

The Ovaro balked but only momentarily. Rock ramparts rose on either side. Fargo could not help feeling hemmed in, and it wasn't a feeling he liked. A lone rifleman on top could keep out an army. He negotiated a series of sharp turns and came to an open space some twenty feet in diameter.

A horse was there, its reins dangling. It raised its head but didn't whinny.

Fargo drew rein and swung down. Boot prints led into a shoulder-wide cleft. He cautiously crept along it until he heard someone cough.

Peering past the next bend, Fargo discovered that the cleft ended amid tall boulders. A gangly man in dark clothes and a dark hat was hunkered on his haunches, a rifle across his legs, staring toward the trading post and the emigrants.

Fargo pressed the Henry's muzzle to the nape of the man's neck. "Nice little hideaway you have here."

The man stiffened and started to rise but thought better of it and froze. "You're good, mister. Damn good. I never heard you sneak up on me."

"That was the general idea." Fargo sidled to where he could reach around and take the man's rifle. Then he relieved him of a Remington revolver and stood back. "Which one are you? Dixon, Preston, or Thorn?"

"You're so damn smart, you figure it out."

"Thorn." Backing up, Fargo placed the other rifle and the revolver at the base of the cliff. Suddenly, without warning, he took a swift step and kicked Thorn in the chest, spilling him in the dust.

Cursing savagely, Thorn spun, "What the hell did you do that for?"

"For trying to kill the Yager woman and me," Fargo said. "Now suppose you tell me what you and your friends are up to?"

"Go to hell."

"You first," Fargo said, and kicked him in the knee.

Hissing through clenched teeth, Thorn clutched his leg with both hands and rolled back and forth. It was a couple of minutes before he stopped and spewed a string of obscenities.

"I think you're after the wagon train," Fargo said when the cursing stopped. "You aim to steal all their valuables. Only you have a problem."

"What would that be?" Thorn spat.

"Me. I thought of it first," Fargo bluffed. "Tell Dix and the rest to stay away. These emigrants are mine."

"*You're* threatening *us*?" Thorn struggled into a sitting position. "We can make coyote food out of you without half trying."

"I won't die easy," Fargo said, "and I'll take more than a few of you with me." He backed toward the cleft.

"You have no idea what you're up against, Flint," Thorn said. "We outnumber you ten to one and that doesn't include the boss."

So there were more of them than he thought, Fargo realized. Enough to ambush a middling-sized wagon train, from the sound of things.

"This won't be the first wagon train we've taken," Thorn unwittingly confirmed. "And if you're not careful, we'll bury you with the rest of those peckerwoods."

"You're welcome to try. Just be sure and tell your boss that I won't take it kindly." Fargo kept Thorn covered until a turn hid him, then he whirled and ran to the Ovaro. He had played his part. Now it was up to the outlaws.

Colonel McCormack was the architect of the plan. As the colonel had explained it that day in his office, "Wagon trains don't just vanish. Someone is behind it. We suspect an outlaw gang. I advise you, therefore, to go in as someone you're not."

"You've lost me," Fargo had admitted.

Colonel McCormack opened a desk drawer and took out a penny dreadful and laid it on the desk facing Fargo so he could read the cover. In bold black letters above an artist's rendering of a granite-faced frontiersman in violent battle with a horde of bloodthirsty Indians was the sensational blurb "Yet another sterling adventure of the Trailsman! Read the latest exploits of the Scout Supreme of the Plains!"

Fargo had squirmed in his chair. "So? I have no control over what those hacks write."

"So whether you like it or not, drivel like this has made you fairly famous. Anyone out here for any length of time is bound to have heard about you, and to know you work for the army on occasion. One mention of your real name and the outlaws we're after will make themselves scarce. We don't want that. We want to flush them out into the open so you can deal with them as you see fit."

So it was that Fargo was calling himself Flint and pretending to be a hard case. Soon, if all went well, he would flush the killers out into the open. Then all he had to do was stop them from killing anyone else without getting himself killed.

At ten to one odds, that was easier said than done.

14

The twang of the fiddle carried on the night air. So did the laughter and happy babble of conversation.

Lanterns had been hung at both ends of the porch, another near the door. Jurgensen was by the steps, smoothly stroking the bow to his fiddle and tapping his foot in time to the music. Couples were spinning and dipping in zestful cheer, their woes and cares forgotten. Others clapped their hands in encouragement. Several jugs were in evidence. Younger children skipped about at play while their older siblings watched the adults, too shy to take part but dearly yearning to do so.

Fargo saw it all from the darkness beyond the circle of lantern light. Sarah and Mandy were with another woman and her children. Jared and Melissa were dancing but Melissa did not appear to be enjoying herself. Granny was in her rocking chair, a smiling spectator.

Reining wide so they wouldn't notice him, Fargo came to the side of the trading post and reined up in the shadows. His bedroll was where he had left it. Dismounting, he removed his saddle and bridle. As tired as he was, it would not be hard to get to sleep. He was about to turn in but a golden-haired vision of loveliness wreathed by lilac perfume had other notions.

"I've been waiting for you," Cathy Fox said. "Where did you get to?"

"Nowhere special," Fargo said.

Cathy glanced at his blankets. "Aren't you joining us?"

"I hadn't planned to." Fargo wanted to be well rested in the morning. He suspected that whatever fate befell the other wagon trains would befall this one somewhere between the trading post and the Sierra Nevadas.

"I haven't danced with anyone all evening," Cathy said. "I was hoping to spend it with you."

"I'm here now." Fargo could tell she was not going to go anywhere so he unfurled and stretched.

"I should be mad at what you did to my brother but Granny says you weren't to blame. That it was her granddaughter who goaded him on and caused all the trouble." Cathy touched his cheek. "Thank you for not hurting him."

"He thinks he's in love."

"I know." Cathy scowled. "I've tried to talk some sense into him but he refuses to listen." She gazed toward the front of the trading post where a few of the dancers were visible. "Jared is planning to ask that trollop to be his wife sometime tonight, if you can believe it."

"I wouldn't worry she'll say yes," Fargo said.

"All that worries me is how crushed he will be when she turns him down," Cathy mentioned. "As brothers go, I have no complaints, and it would sadden me to see him sad."

"He's a grown man," Fargo said, "and some lessons are only learned the hard way."

"Is that the voice of experience speaking?"

Fargo fished in his saddlebag and held out his whiskey bottle. "Care for a swig?"

"Thank you, no. I'm not as fond of seeing double as you are."

Fargo put the bottle back.

Tilting her face to the sparkling stars, Cathy took a much deeper breath than she needed to, so that her large breasts swelled to even larger proportions. "It's a gorgeous night for a walk, wouldn't you say?"

"Was that a hint?" Fargo had to grin. The varied and devious ploys women used were unending.

"If you care to construe it as one," Cathy parried, and offered her arm. "No true gentleman would refuse."

"I'm no gentleman." But Fargo took her arm anyway and they strolled past the fence and gate and off across the grassy field, away from the music and everyone else and possible prying eyes.

"Exactly *what* you are, I haven't quite made up my mind yet," Cathy commented. "But you're not as mean as you make yourself out to be."

"You couldn't convince Peter Sloane of that."

"He thinks you're the devil incarnate," Cathy said. "He asked Granny to run you off but she refused. My woman's intuition tells me she's fond of you, for some strange reason." At that Cathy laughed.

Fargo liked how her blond hair shimmered in the moonlight. He also liked the saucy sway to her hips. She was enormously attractive, this farmer's daughter. Below his belt stirring began.

"Melissa is another story," Cathy was saying. "She hates you. I saw it in her eyes. Don't turn your back on her or you'll regret it."

Stands of trees appeared, islands in the night.

"How long do you intend to stay with the wagon train?" Cathy inquired.

"Are you asking? Or is Sloane?"

"How did you know? He came up to me a while ago and asked me and I answered him truthfully and said I have no idea," Cathy related. "But I would like to, for my own sake, not for his peace of mind."

"I'll be with you as long as it takes," Fargo said.

"As long as what takes, exactly?" When he didn't answer, Cathy said, "At moments like these I wonder if my trust in you is misplaced. It's dangerous for a woman to think with her heart instead of her head."

Fargo glanced over his shoulder but did not see anyone trailing them. Ahead and to the right a hundred yards were the boulders screening Thorn, if he was still there. Fargo bore to the left.

"I doubt anyone will miss me," Cathy informed him. "The women are all having fun and the men are well on their way to being tipsy. By midnight I daresay most will be drunk." She giggled. "I can't wait to see their expressions tomorrow when their heads are splitting."

"I know how that feels," Fargo remarked.

Cathy studied him a moment. "Do you have any idea what to expect on the next leg of our journey?"

"More of what you've been through already."

"Mrs. Jurgensen and Mrs. Nickelby are worried, and I can't say as I blame them. The unknown is always scary."

"You'll reach California," Fargo said, his conscience pricking him. Who was he to say *any* of them would?

They strolled past several more stands, Cathy deep in thought. The canyon walls echoed to the revelry, and even though they were fifty yards from the trading post, it seemed as if they were right there among them.

Jurgensen began playing a slow song, and Cathy stopped and turned and held out her arms. "Care to dance?"

"Here?" Fargo would rather do what they came to

do, but he indulged her whim. Holding her at arm's length, as was the fashion, he slowly whirled her in wide circles, her dress switching in the high grass.

Closing her eyes, Cathy drifted with the music. "My mother taught me to dance when I was seven, and we would go to church socials and the like. But I rarely get to indulge these days."

Fargo couldn't remember the last time he was at a dance.

"It's too bad moments like these can't last forever. I am enjoying myself immensely, Mr. Flint."

"Good." Fargo would enjoy himself more doing something else but he kept on spinning her until the song ended.

"Thank you, kind sir," Cathy said, sliding her elbow through his. "Where to now?"

Fargo made for the farthest group of cottonwoods. It would afford the most privacy.

Leaning against him, Cathy sighed. "Have you ever met someone you thought would make a wonderful wife but destiny conspired to separate you?"

Where that came from, Fargo could only guess. He changed the subject. "From here on out always keep a gun handy. The Paiutes might try to take a woman next time."

"You're worried about me? I'm touched."

"I just don't want to wear my horse out going after you."

"Sure, Mr. Flint. Sure."

A few moments more and they were in the cottonwoods, in darkest shadow. Fargo stopped and pressed against her and cupped her bottom. "Did you say something about touching?" he grinned.

Her mouth rose to his in a lingering, exquisite kiss. "Mmmmmm," she cooed when she pulled back for breath. "That was nice. Very nice. Something tells me you've had a lot of practice. Is that true?"

There were questions no man should answer and that was one. Fargo kissed her again, sliding his hands up her back and across her thighs to her flat belly. She gave a sharp intake of breath when he cupped her breasts. With his right hand he aroused her while with his left he undid buttons and pried at stays. Soon her wonderful globes burst free. They were huge. Pendulous melons tipped by nipples as hard as nails. He inhaled one and rimmed it with his tongue and she arched her back and gasped.

"Yes! I like that!"

So did Fargo. He squeezed one breast and then the other. He nuzzled his face between them and licked her silken smooth skin in small swirls until he was at her nipple again.

Cathy delicately ran a fingernail along his neck to the underside of his chin and tugged at his beard.

Kissing her throat and then her shoulder, Fargo remembered to stay vigilant. He scanned the trees and the undergrowth but did not see anyone.

"Is something wrong?" Cathy asked.

Fargo placed his hands on her slim waist, lifted her off the ground, and backed her against a tree. Sculpting his hard body to hers, he hitched at her dress until he had it high enough to explore her undergarments. His mouth strayed to her neck and he nibbled and licked.

Meanwhile Cathy's left hand fell to his gun belt. She loosened it enough for it to slide down his legs. It ended up around Fargo's ankles. He tried to kick free but the belt snagged on his spurs. Bending, he slid it off, then straightened and stiffened in pleasure when her hand enfolded his pole. In an instant he was hard and erect.

"My, my," Cathy grinned. "You remind me of that stallion our neighbor had. I can't wait to have you inside me."

Farm girls, experience had taught Fargo, were marvelously frank about their physical needs, and she was no exception.

Cathy rubbed him up and down, saying, "I should warn you. I bite when I'm excited."

"Do tell." Fargo had been with more women than most. Tall, short, blondes, brunettes, redheads. Young and not-so-young. City girls and their country cousins. Indian maidens and white doves. They could all be broken down into two groups: those who lay there like bumps on a log and let the man do all the work, and those who let themselves be caught up in the carnal pleasure of things.

Cathy Fox was one of the latter. Her lips and hands were everywhere, touching, stroking, inciting ripples of delight. She freed his manhood and rubbed and squeezed until he thought he would explode, then she cupped him, lower down, taxing his self-control to the limit.

Suddenly sliding his arm under her legs, Fargo lowered her to the ground. The high grass hid them. He brushed a finger across her slit and her nails dug deep into his shoulders. She was wet for him, her thighs drenched. With his middle finger he lightly flicked her swollen knob.

"Ohhhhhh, Flint," Cathy breathed, and pressed her face against his shoulder to smother more moans.

Fargo moved his finger over her. That was all it took for her to clamp her thighs to his hand and grind against him in unrestrained release. She came, and came again, in great shudders, but she did not cry out. Only after she crested did she whisper, "I never— I never—"

Kissing her, Fargo tasted blood. She had bit her lip so hard, she broke the skin. That did not stop her from mashing her mouth against his and trying to suck his tongue down her throat. Her nails pricked the nape of his neck, her hips were in constant motion.

How long they lay there, Fargo couldn't rightly say. They were both hot and panting when he finally spread her legs wide and rubbed his member where she wanted it most. She surprised him by reaching down and slowly feeding him into her until, with a quick grind of her hips, the deed was done. He was buried to the hilt.

For a while they lay still, only their mouths and tongues working. Then Fargo's hands rose to her breasts and hers lowered to hold him in her palms. He felt the pressure of her ankles against the small of his back.

"Now," Cathy said. "Please now."

It would not take much to send Fargo over the edge. When Cathy squeezed him with her inner walls, the inevitable took place. Gripping her hips, he rammed into her. It triggered her own release. Her body came off the ground and she met each thrust with a matching one of her own. Harder and harder and faster and faster they went. Then, suddenly clinging to his chest, Cathy moaned and gushed.

At length they lay side by side, breathing heavily, Fargo grateful for the breeze. He closed his eyes, content to stay there a while, but the soft scrape of a shoe or boot instantly galvanized him into sitting up.

Off in the dark someone or something moved.

Bending, Fargo whispered in Cathy's ear, "We have company. Don't make a sound." Hastily dressing, he strapped on his gun belt, palmed his Colt, and slunk toward the edge of the stand.

Cathy had rearranged her dress and was right behind him, buttoning the last of her buttons.

Once more a shoe scuffed the ground, and a figure took shape. A figure Fargo recognized. He let her come within a dozen paces, then demanded, "What are you doing out here?"

Granny Barnes gave a start. Her hand swooped to the Walker Colt but she didn't draw it. "Mr. Flint!" she exclaimed. "You about scared me out of a year's growth, and at my age I can't afford to lose a single day!"

Fargo strode out from under the trees. "You haven't answered me."

"I'm looking for that darned granddaughter of mine." Granny saw Cathy, and grinned. "Well, well. You must be made of honey, the way the ladies have a hankering for your company."

"What's this about Melissa?" Cathy asked.

"She went off with your brother a while ago and they haven't come back yet," Granny said.

"Uh oh," Cathy said.

"What's the matter, Miss Fox?"

Before another word could be said, the canyon rocked to the blast of gunfire.

15

Fargo reached the front of the trading post first, his Colt in hand, expecting to find the emigrants under attack. Instead, he beheld Peter Sloane and Nickelby and several others firing into the air. They were drunk. So silly with drink, they giggled and tittered and clapped one another on the back at their antics.

"There's the North Star!" Sloane bawled. "I'll try for it." And so saying, he took aim and fired, then cackled uproariously. "Dang me! Look, boys. It's still there. I must have missed."

"My turn," Nickelby said, and aimed at another twinkling celestial light. His rifle spat smoke and lead and he laughed and smacked his leg. "I hope I used enough powder!"

Fargo slid the Colt into his holster. The music had stopped and some of the women were standing about chatting. Others were ushering children to their wagons to tuck them in.

Cathy caught up, nearly breathless. "Is that all it is? Those fools and their silly antics?"

Granny came puffing out of the dark. For her age she was spry. "Look at them!" she snapped. "For two bits I'd take a bullwhip to the whole bunch. They can hardly stand up straight, they've drunk so much."

Peter Sloane heard her and tottered toward them.

"There you are! Care to shoot a star out of the sky, Granny?"

"I'd like to break that rifle over your head," she rejoined. "Stop all that racket this instant."

"We're just having a little fun," Sloane protested. "Where's the harm?"

"Who knows who might be out there listening?" Granny said.

Pouting like a small boy whose wrist had been slapped for misbehaving, Sloane declared, "It's not as if the Paiutes don't know where to find you. Or are you thinking of someone else?"

"Out here one never knows," Granny said, and gestured. "It's plain you don't give a fig about your wives and kids."

"Now see here," Sloane said.

"No, you see here," Granny barked, poking him. "Your shindig is over as of this minute. Off to bed with the lot of you, and I don't want to hear another peep until tomorrow."

Sloane was inclined to argue but his wife came over and took him by the arm. "Mrs. Barnes is right, dear. We'd better turn in if we want to get an early start in the morning."

Several of the men grumbled but when Sloane staggered toward his wagon, the rest took that as their cue to do likewise.

"Now that the ruckus is over, I'm off to bed too," Granny said. "I have a busy day ahead of me tomorrow."

That left Fargo and Cathy. She glanced toward Sarah's wagon as if to assure herself Sarah wasn't watching, then rose on the tips of her toes and pecked him on the cheek. "Any time you have a hankering," she huskily whispered, and pranced off humming.

Fargo had not seen any sign of Jared. He debated

hunting for him but decided not to, not after Jared's antics earlier. Soon he was spread out on his blankets, reflecting on all that had happened since he hooked up with the wagon train. While he had uncovered a few pieces to the puzzle, others remained elusive.

That was Fargo's last thought before drifting off. A light sleeper, he awoke twice. Once a vague sound was to blame. He sat up, his hand drifting to the Henry, but the sound wasn't repeated. The second time was shortly before dawn. The sky was brightening when the Ovaro nickered and Fargo rolled onto his side to find out why and found himself staring into the barrel of a rifle held by Thorn.

"You're not the only one good at sneaking up on folks."

Shorty came from behind him. "We're supposed to take you alive, Flint. Which is too bad. If it were up to me, you'd never have woke up."

"But we have to do as we're told," said a third man, and from over by the fence came Swink. Careful not to step between Fargo and Thorn's rifle, he took the Henry and the Colt and gave them to Shorty. "Surprised to see me?"

"Not really," Fargo said. He had suspected all along that Swink was working with the outlaws.

Swink beckoned to someone else. "We have him. It was easier than we thought it would be."

"Aren't they all?" said one of four men who came out of the dark. His voice pegged him as Dixon. With him were Preston and two others Fargo never saw before. But that wasn't all. On their heels padded four swarthy, muscular figures, three of whom moved with the fluid grace of cats. The fourth had a pronounced limp and a perpetual sneer. Streaks of war paint lent dashes of color.

"Lame Bear," Fargo said.

The Paiute hefted the Sharps Granny had given him in exchange for Mandy. "You hear of me, eh?" He swelled with pride.

"I hear you steal little girls. It takes a brave warrior to do that."

Lame Bear growled and swept the Sharps over his head to bash him in the face but Swink intervened.

"None of that, damn your red hide! Not if you ever want more ammunition." To Fargo Swink said, "On your feet. Put your hands behind your back."

Fargo still had his Arkansas Toothpick in an ankle sheath on his right leg, but he would be riddled before he got it out. Slowly standing, he did as he had been instructed, and Dixon bound his wrists with a short piece of rope.

"We came prepared," Swink bragged.

Shorty stepped up close and gouged the Henry into Fargo's spine. "Not a peep, now, you hear? The sun will be up in a while and we have a surprise to spring."

Fargo was prodded to the corner of the trading post, then had to watch in helpless anger as the others spread out and silently slunk toward the prairie schooners. He yearned to shout a warning, to do *something*.

As if he sensed as much, Shorty warned, "Behave yourself, Flint. We can't have you spoiling things."

Some of the emigrants were asleep in the open, some under their wagons, still others inside. Loud snores drowned out whatever sounds the outlaws and the renegades made. Weapons at the ready, they waited until a budding golden glow gave them ample light to see by.

Peter Sloane was the first to be taken. He was sprawled on his back beside his wagon, a jug upended beside him, his mouth open wide enough for a prairie dog to crawl in, his snores loud enough to be heard in St. Louis. Dixon, Thorn, and Swink surrounded him, and while Thorn kept him covered, Dix clamped a hand over his mouth and jerked him up so that Swink could bind his hands behind his back. It was accomplished in seconds, Sloane so befuddled he offered no resistance. Nor did he think to cry out as Swink was applying a gag.

Sloane's wife and children stirred, and suddenly the Paiutes played their part. Snatching the mother and her offspring, the warriors hauled them to the porch where they were swiftly bound and gagged.

"Pretty slick, huh?" Shorty said. "We have it down pat."

Quietly, methodically, with almost military precision, the rest of the emigrants were taken captive. The men were too hung over to lift a finger to defend themselves or their loved ones until it was too late. One of the women threw back her head to shout but Lame Bear was on her in a heartbeat, his bronzed hand over the lower half of her face.

Only the Yagers and the Jurgensens had slept in their wagons. The sun was up when Sarah climbed from the rear of hers, a bucket in her hand, and was promptly seized. Mandy heard her mother's stifled outcry and poked her head out, right into a Paiute's waiting arms.

The outlaws didn't wait for the Jurgensens to wake up. Dix knocked on the side, saying, "Rise and shine in there!"

"What's that?" Jurgensen sleepily leaned out to see who it was, and was grabbed and wrestled to the ground. Awake in an instant, he struggled, shouting, "Martha! My gun! I need my gun!"

A rifle jutted from the wagon. Mrs. Jurgensen, unaware of how many she was up against, pointed it at Swink, saying, "Release my husband or suffer the consequences!"

Lame Bear motioned at a tall warrior. In a lithe bound the Paiute was on the wagon seat. Another bound, and he was in among the family. Their two children screamed, and then the warrior hauled Mrs. Jurgensen from the wagon. In the blink of an eye she was subdued.

"And that's the last of them," Shorty said, nudging Fargo onto the porch where the emigrants were now trussed up like calves for the slaughter. Their ankles had been bound as well as their wrists, and each one silenced by a gag.

Sarah and Mandy were near the rocking chair, Mandy fearfully huddled against her mother. Cathy was by herself, sitting straight and tall. Of Jared there was no sign.

Dixon and the others gathered by the steps. Lame Bear and his renegades squatted well back, their arms across their knees, as inscrutable as statues.

"What now?" Fargo asked Shorty. "Do you line us up and execute us or give us to the Paiutes?"

"You think you have it all figured out, but you don't," Shorty said.

The front door opened and out stepped Granny, her big Walker Colt in her hands. "What have we here?" she demanded, and grinned. "Well done, Dixon. I couldn't be more proud of you boys if I tried."

"Thank you, Grandma," Dix said.

"Grandma?" Fargo repeated.

Granny Barnes sat in her rocking chair and placed the Walker Colt in her lap. "You don't see the resemblance? About the eyes and the chin? His full name is Dixon Barnes. He's the oldest of the brood. Preston, Shorty, Zeke, Caleb, they're all my grandsons. Not Mr. Swink, though. His last name is Gattes. I pay him to use his silver tongue to lure the wagon trains here."

The sheer diabolical deviltry of her scheme slowly sank in. Fargo wanted to beat his head against the porch post for not realizing the truth sooner.

"Don't forget Raskum," Shorty said bitterly.

"Ah, yes." Granny clucked like a biddy hen. "He never could listen, never do exactly as I told him, and now he's maggot bait."

Shorty jabbed Fargo. "Thanks to this gob of spit. I say we pour dirt down his throat until he chokes to death."

Granny's eyes acquired a steely cast. "Since when do you give the orders around here, grandson?"

"It was just an idea."

"When I want a suggestion from you I'll ask for one," Granny said curtly. To Fargo she said, "What do you think of our flytrap, Mr. Flint?"

"How long have you been doing this?" Fargo asked so she wouldn't suspect how much he knew.

"This makes the fifth wagon train in two years. I always wait until the night before they plan to pull out and let them have all the free whiskey they can drink. It makes the job a lot easier."

Fargo nodded at the trading post. "All this just so you can steal people blind?"

"Just so we can steal folks blind, yes."

"There is no Barnes Trail?"

"Never was, never will be."

"All the trade goods inside are from the other wagon trains?"

"You catch on quick," Granny complimented him. "Their money and jewelry and whatnot are in the root cellar. Another two or three wagon trains and we'll have enough to live in grand style wherever we want."

"Why are you telling me this?" Fargo wondered.

"You impress me, Mr. Flint. Mr. Raskum always fancied himself fast with a pistol but you're faster or you wouldn't be here. How would you like to replace him?"

Shorty forgot himself and took a step. "You can't be serious, Grandma! He's the one who *killed* Raskum."

"What better proof that he's the better man?" Granny asked.

"Raskum and me were friends," Shorty objected. "It doesn't seem right, us working with the hombre who blew out his wick."

Thorn moved onto the porch, "I agree with Shorty, Grandma. This bastard snuck up behind me and damn near stove in my ribs."

"But he didn't kill you," Granny debated them. "He left you alive to relay a warning. Which shows me he's smart as well as tough, and we can always use a man who uses his head."

"I don't trust him," Thorn said.

Shorty wasn't done complaining either. "Aren't you forgetting something, Grandma?" He touched his bandaged shoulder. "This bastard put a slug through me. Your own kin. Maybe you can forget that but I sure as hell can't."

"I'll thank you to watch your tone, young man," Granny scolded. "And no, I haven't forgotten. But the fact he didn't shoot you dead when he could have tells me he's not trigger-happy, which was another fault of the late Ira Raskum."

Dixon had been studying Fargo since the argument began. Now he commented, "I've never doubted you, Grandma. You know that. But I've got an uneasy feeling about this one. How can we be sure he won't turn on us?"

Granny smiled. "By putting him to a test."

"It better be a good one," Dix said.

Shifting in her chair, Granny pointed at Mandy. "Take that child ten steps from the porch and leave her there."

Fargo's gut balled into a knot.

A cry of despair tore from Sarah's throat as three of the Barnes converged. She reared up and tried to butt Dixon but Zeke and Caleb held her while Dixon picked up a struggling Mandy and carried her the required distance.

The child lay sobbing in the dirt and looking in mute appeal to her horror-struck mother.

"Now what?" Shorty asked.

"Why, it's simple," Granny responded. "We cut Flint loose, we give him a gun, and he shoots her."

16

Skye Fargo had guessed what Grandma Barnes had in her devious mind before her own grandsons did. He was beginning to understand just how unbelievably vicious the seemingly sweet and kindly woman truly was. Now, as Thorn and Preston trained rifles on him and Shorty drew a folding knife and cut the rope that bound his wrists, he racked his brain for a way out of the corner Granny had boxed him in.

"All you have to do to prove yourself is walk over to that cute little child and blow her sweet young brains out." Granny wagged the Walker Colt. "You can use my pistol."

Tears were streaming down Mandy's face.

Sarah was striving fiercely to break free of Zeke and Caleb but they held fast to her arms. The rest of the emigrants could do nothing, not bound as they were and covered by the Barnes clan.

Granny began unloading the Walker. "In case my grandsons are right about you, Mr. Flint, I'm only leaving one cartridge in the cylinder. That's all you need to get the job done."

"What does shooting a kid prove?" Fargo tried to dissuade her.

"Where your true sentiments lie," Granny said. "If you're cut from the same cloth we are, killing her should be easy as can be. The Paiutes could do it. My grandsons could do it. *I* could do it. Now prove to us you can."

Shorty pushed Fargo toward the rocking chair. "Get moving. And remember. One wrong move and the buzzards will feast on your carcass."

Fargo threaded through the sprawled emigrants. All eyes were on him. Some, like Sloane's, were filled with hate. Some, like Jurgensen's, were mirrors of worry. Only Sarah and Cathy suspected the truth, and their eyes were pools of sympathy.

To stall, Fargo asked, "Is this how you'll dispose of the rest? Shoot them one by one?"

"Oh please," Granny said. "Give me more credit than that. Bullet holes are dead giveaways. If the army ever found the remains, they would know foul play was involved. No, I have a much more practical method." She laughed sadistically. "We'll do as we did with the pilgrims from the other wagon trains. We'll take them and their wagons off into the middle of nowhere and leave them to die of thirst and hunger. Everyone will think their own stupidity killed them. That they tried to find a new route to California and never made it."

"With their hands tied behind their backs and gags in their mouths?"

Granny made that clucking sound again. "How stupid do you think I am, Mr. Flint? After they die, my grandsons take the ropes and the gags. There's no evidence of wrongdoing so no one will ever be the wiser."

"And you keep whatever is valuable."

"For goods for the trading post. Exactly. The rest of their belongings stay in the wagons."

Shorty snickered. "My grandma has it all figured out. She's smarter than you and me and all these sheep combined."

Fargo had to admit their scheme was well planned. "What do you do with the animals? Leave them to die too?"

"Some," Granny said. "Some go to Lame Bear. He's becoming a rich man by Paiute standards thanks to me."

A thought struck Fargo as he glanced at the renegades. "You had him steal Mandy on purpose, didn't you?"

Granny chuckled and winked at her grandsons. "What did I tell you, boys? This one is mighty clever." She nodded. "I have Lame Bear steal a child from all the wagon trains and bring the kids to me. That way, when the emigrants show up, they think I've done them a big favor. Makes it easy to earn their trust."

Peter Sloane angrily sat up and managed to spit out the strip of cloth that had been shoved in his mouth. "You're a fiend, woman! How can you do this to innocent men, women, and children?"

"There aren't any of us innocent, Mr. Sloane," Granny rebutted. "But to answer your question, I do it because I can. Because I like to. Because it beats having to work for a living."

"You would rather practice deceit and murder than live by the honest sweat of your brow?" Sloane railed. "What kind of monster are you?"

Dixon went to strike him with a rifle butt but Granny shook her head. She was quiet a while, then she said, "I'll do you the courtesy of answering you honestly, Mr. Sloane."

"Why should I believe you when everything else you've told us was a bald-faced lie?"

"Not everything, Mr. Sloane," Granny said. "But maybe I'm expecting too much. You'll never understand because you don't think right."

"Me?" The farmer was incredulous.

"Yes. You. Like a lot of people, you think everyone

should think the same way you do. You think they should believe the same things. Do the same things. But that's not how life is. What seems wrong to you can seem perfectly natural to someone else."

Sloane snorted in contempt. "You're bandying words. Wrong is wrong and right is right and that's all there is to it."

Again Granny was quiet a bit. "Mr. Sloane, when my daughter and her husband died, I was left with eight mouths to feed, counting my own. Jobs for women are scarce. Jobs that pay well enough to feed and clothe a family our size are even scarcer. I had to make do the best I could."

"So you embarked on a spree of murder and robbery?"

"We lived in Indiana at the time. We were wearing rags and short on food. One day a man and his wife stopped at our farm and asked for water. They were on their way west in a covered wagon. I told him he could have all he wanted for fifty cents. Fifty measly cents. But do you know what he did? He cursed me and insulted me. He said he had never heard of anyone charging for water before. He went on and on until I couldn't take it anymore and I took my squirrel gun from inside the house and shot him dead. Then I had to shoot his wife when she came at me with a carving knife."

"How horrible."

"How enlightening," Granny said. "Their wagon was loaded with things we could use. Clothes. Furniture. Food. It gave me a lot to think about. That night I buried the bodies and we loaded up our few effects and off we went. From time to time we killed a few other folks, just to get by. We were at Fort Bridger when I got the idea of setting up my own trading post and came up with the story of the Barnes Trail as bait."

"You are scum, woman! You and this whole evil family of yours. You deserve nothing less than to be strung up by the neck."

"Some people don't have the intelligence of a turnip," Granny said testily. "Shut him up, Dix."

Sloane tried to roll aside but Dixon was on him in a twinkling. The rifle descended, there was the sound of wood connecting with flesh and bone, and Sloane slumped to the porch.

Granny turned. "Now then, Mr. Flint, where were we? Is there anything else you would like to know?"

Fargo shook his head. He had learned all he needed to, and then some.

"Then let's get on with it, shall we?" Granny held the Walker Colt out to him. "Here you go."

Just then the trading post door opened and out shuffled Melissa. She was half-awake, her hair tousled, her feet bare. Stifling a yawn, she gazed disinterestedly at the prone forms all around her. "You started without me, Grandma."

"What else did you expect, you lazy layabout," Granny replied. "You sleep more than anyone I know."

"Don't start," Melissa said.

Granny was growing impatient. "What are you waiting for, Mr. Flint? If you want to join our enterprise, take this and get it over with."

The Walker was twice as heavy as Fargo's own revolver. The instant he touched it, Shorty, Dix, Thorn, and Preston trained rifles on him. He avoided looking at Sarah as he went down the steps and over to where Mandy was weeping and sniffling. She gazed up at him, at the revolver, but she did not show the least bit of fear.

"I have ten dollars that says he won't do it," Thorn said.

"I'll take that bet," Swink spoke up. "I was there when he killed Raskum. He's as cold-blooded as they come."

Fargo pointed the Walker at Mandy's forehead and curled his thumb around the hammer. He had made a decision. As every frontiersman learned, the most effective way to kill a snake was to chop off its head. Grandma Barnes was the head of the clan. She was the brains of the bunch. Without her, the rest might take to bickering and fighting amongst themselves. Perhaps even break up. It would cost him his life to kill her but it might bring an end to the murders.

"Well?" Granny goaded. "What in tarnation are you waiting for, Mr. Flint? The girl to pull the trigger herself?"

"My name isn't Flint," Fargo said.

"No? Then what is it?"

"Skye Fargo. I was sent by the army to ferret you out. A patrol will be here tomorrow or the next day to check on this wagon train." Fargo's mix of truth and lie produced the result he intended: it shocked them so much, they were a shade slow in reacting when he raised the Walker Colt and fired at Granny's chest. He had her dead to rights. The slug should have cored her heart and left her pumping her life's blood out on the porch. But no shot rang out. There was a *click*, and that was all.

"Damn you!" Thorn raged, taking a bead.

"No!" Granny hollered. "Whoever shoots him will answer to me." Rising, she walked out from under the overhang. "My revolver, if you please, Mr. Fargo." She accepted it and opened her other palm to show the bullets she had removed. "I took them all."

"You didn't trust me after all," Fargo said.

"I trust no one until they prove they deserve it." Granny started reloading. "But that's not important right now. What is important is the claim you just made. You're really Skye Fargo? The one folks say can track an ant over solid rock?"

Thorn did not wait for Fargo's answer. "He's trying to trick us, Grandma. Say the word and his fooling days are over."

"Not so fast," Granny cautioned. "We can't dismiss him out of hand. The army was bound to investigate the disappearances sooner or later."

"So they sent one man instead of a whole company?" Shorty said. "I'm not buying it."

"If that one man is the best there is at what he does, it makes sense," Granny replied. She walked in a slow circle around Fargo, her chin bowed. When she was once again in front of him, she straightened. "Even if he is who he claims, we stick to our original plan. Only now we have one more to kill."

"And if the army does come?" from Preston.

"They'll find me in my rocking chair, knitting," Granny said. "The rest of you will lie low until they're gone." She turned to Melissa. "Except for you. You'll charm whoever is in charge into thinking you're the cat's meow and keep his mind off why he's here."

"I am quite the charmer, aren't I?" Melissa boasted. "You should have seen the look on that farmer last night when I told him I would never marry someone so dull and dumb." She scanned the emigrants. "Where is he, anyway?"

"Who?" Granny said.

"Jared Fox. The jackass who proposed to me." Melissa pointed at Cathy. "There's his sister but I don't see any sign of him."

"One of them is missing?" Granny spun toward the Paiutes. "Did you hear that, Lame Bear? What are you waiting for? Find him, and find him quick!"

Lame Bear addressed the other warriors in their

own tongue and they loped to the prairie schooners and began going from wagon to wagon.

Granny hustled onto the porch. Removing Cathy's gag, she demanded, "Where's your brother, missy?"

"I don't know. He never came back last night."

Gripping her arm, Granny twisted until Cathy cried out. "The truth, damn you, or by God I'll cut out your tongue!"

"I'm telling you the truth!" Cathy cried. "I stayed up late waiting for him but I fell asleep. The next thing I knew, your grandsons were hauling me from our wagon and tying me up."

Granny muttered and turned to her granddaughter. "The devil take you and your carnal urges! You broke that boy's heart so he wandered off to mope." She scanned the canyon. "He's probably out there somewhere right this second, watching us."

"Don't fret, Grandma," Dixon said. "The savages will find him."

"We can't rely on them," Granny said. "Not if the army is on its way." She pondered a few moments. "Tie Fargo and put him on the porch with the rest. Melissa and I will stand guard while you boys go help Lame Bear."

"All of us?" Thorn said.

"What's the matter? Did you break your legs?" Granny was growing mad. "Yes, by heaven, *all of you*! Check behind every boulder, every bush. In every tree, every crevice. Move it!"

Shorty pushed Fargo over onto the porch and shoved him to his knees, then covered him while Dixon retied his wrists and bound his ankles. When Dix was done they ran to aid the rest.

Granny moved her rocking chair to the edge of the porch so she could watch the search unfold. "This is what comes of not listening to me," she said to her granddaughter. "I told you that your shenanigans would cause trouble one day."

"I'm not in the mood for another of your lectures." Melissa opened the door. "After I eat I'll come out and spell you."

"Don't bother."

"What about the girl?" Fargo asked. Mandy was still lying out in the dirt. She had stopped crying and was gazing longingly at her mother.

"What about her?" Granny snapped. "She can bake under the sun for all I care!" Swiveling, she leveled the Walker. "As for you, I don't much like being made a fool of. It makes me look bad in front of my grandchildren. After we find Jared Fox, I'm going to make an example of you. I'm going to give you to the Paiutes to torture right here in front of everyone. It will be fun to watch."

17

Fargo lay with his back propped against the roughhewn logs of the trading post wall and his legs bent slightly to one side. He watched the Paiutes leap from the last wagon and dart into the woods like starved wolves eager for the scent of prey. Several of the Barnes brothers had already gone off down the canyon. The rest had gone up it. With Melissa banging pots and pans inside, only Granny was left to guard them and she had her back to him and was slowly rocking in her chair. The Walker Colt was in her lap and she had resumed her knitting.

By shifting his broad shoulders, Fargo was able to touch his spurs. They were sharp enough to eventually saw through the rope but he did not have the luxury of time. Instead, he stretched his arms further and slid his fingers under his right boot. He could reach the hilt of the Arkansas Toothpick but he couldn't draw it from its sheath. The rope around his ankles was too tight.

Peter Sloane saw what he was doing and suddenly crawled toward the rocking chair. "Granny, a word with you, if you please."

For a harrowing few seconds Fargo thought Sloane intended to tell her, perhaps in exchange for his own life.

"What do you want?" Granny harshly demanded.

Sloane glanced at Fargo and smiled and bobbed his chin, then wriggled still closer to the chair. "To reason with you."

Belatedly, Fargo realized Sloane was distracting her for his benefit. He pried at the knots with his fingernails.

"Save your breath," Granny said. "There's nothing you can say that will make me change my mind. I've heard it all before."

Sloane pleaded with her anyway, going on and on about an army patrol the wagon train encountered soon after leaving Fort Bridger, and how the captain of the patrol would wonder what had happened to them.

Fargo barely listened. He was tugging and tearing at the knots and the rope in a desperate bid to loosen them. His fingers hurt like hell but he stuck with it. The lives of everyone depended on him and him alone, and he would not let them down.

Sarah and Cathy and some of the others were staring expectantly, and Fargo wished they wouldn't. Granny might notice and come over to find out what he was up to, dashing any hope they had.

Sloane switched to a different appeal. "What kind of woman are you that you can kill children and infants? You've had children of your own. You're a grandmother. It flies in the face of human nature."

"What do you know?" Granny hissed. "It's not as if I put a gun to their heads. Starvation kills them. I'm not even there when they breathe their last."

"I see. So long as you don't witness their deaths, you can live with yourself?" Peter Sloane said, his loathing transparent.

"Shut up, farmer. You're so ignorant, it's pitiful. You don't know me. You only think you do."

Sloane glanced at Fargo, saw he was still striving to

142

loosen the rope, and crawled nearer yet to the rocking chair. "The lives of my wife and my children mean too much to me. Please. I beseech you. Call off this madness. Surely you have a shred of decency left somewhere inside you?"

"You couldn't be more wrong if you tried," Granny said, and was out of the rocking chair and on him in two swift steps. In her right hand was a knitting needle which she plunged into Sloane's right eye. He made a gurgling noise and jerked back but she grabbed the back of his head with her other hand and shoved the needle in deeper.

Muffled cries and screams came from Sloane's wife and son and daughter as Sloane broke into convulsions and flopped wildly about. Gradually his movements ceased and his body went limp, red rivulets seeping from his ruined eye.

Breathing heavily, Granny coldly regarded her handiwork. "I warned him," she said to none of them in particular. "I told him to shut up but he wouldn't listen."

Fargo had frozen when the rest did but not for the same reason. He tensed when Granny glanced in his direction but she did not notice his hands. She kicked Sloane in the face, then sat in the rocking chair. As soon as her back was to him once again, he renewed his assault on the stubborn knots. Two of the three were slowly loosening. But it was taking much too long. At any moment some of Granny's brood or the Paiutes might return, and that would be that.

Sloane's wife and children were crying their hearts out, the daughter sobbing in great heaves. Granny kept looking at them and finally shook her other knitting needle at Sloane's wife.

"Quit your blubbering, damn it! Quiet your brats or I'll do it for you."

Unable to speak or use her hands, Mrs. Sloane

nudged her daughter with her head but the girl could not stop bawling.

One of the knots came undone. Fargo tried to draw the Toothpick but the rope still wasn't loose enough. He resumed prying at the second knot, prying so hard he nearly tore a fingernail off.

Cathy Fox was the only other emigrant who wasn't gagged, and she attempted to help Mrs. Sloane by urging, "Susan! Tommy! Stop crying! Hold it in for now."

They couldn't. Not with their father lying there with a knitting needle jutting from his ruptured eye. It was asking the impossible. Susan cried all the louder while Tommy started to wriggle toward the body.

"Don't say I didn't warn you," Granny said. Rising, she turned to the children. "Which one should I do first? Daughter or son?"

"In heaven's name, no!" Cathy begged.

Fargo undid the second knot. Wedging his fingers under the rope, he worked them back and forth.

Granny moved toward Susan. Gone was the smiling, kindly face that greeted them upon their arrival. In its place was a twisted mask of hatred and bloodlust. Seizing Susan Sloane by the hair, she jerked the girl's head back, exposing her throat. "What fine white skin you have, little one."

Suddenly the Arkansas Toothpick was in Fargo's hand. Reversing his grip, he sliced at the rope around his wrists. All he needed was another twenty to thirty seconds but he had run out of time.

Granny was poised for a fatal thrust. "Give my regards to your father, child. You'll find him in the part of hell they reserve for really stupid people." She bent the girl's neck a trifle more.

"Noooooo!" Cathy wailed. "You can't! You mustn't! No one can be so cruel!"

"I can, dearie," Granny said.

The rope around Fargo's wrists parted. Heaving onto his knees, he threw the double-edged Toothpick with all the skill and all the strength he possessed.

A gleaming streak of steel lightning struck Grandma Barnes in the throat and jolted her backward. It made her miss her stroke, the needle digging a furrow in Susan's shoulder instead of impaling her through the neck. Letting go of it, Granny clutched at the Arkansas Toothpick, then did the last thing she should do—she yanked the blade out. Blood gushed in a scarlet torrent.

Granny gaped at Fargo. Her mouth moved but no words came out, only inarticulate sounds. She took a step toward the door but that was as far as she got; her legs gave way.

Fargo quickly finished removing the rope around his ankles. He rose just as the trading post door opened.

"Grandma, what's all the commo—" Melissa began, and recoiled, dropping a cup of coffee she held.

Anxious to reach her before she brought the others down on their heads, Fargo lunged. He clamped a hand onto her wrist but she twisted free before he could get a good grip. Whirling, she darted inside, and he went after her. She headed for the counter, reaching it a few steps ahead of him. Her hand ducked underneath and reappeared holding a Remington revolver.

Fargo had to stop her from firing. The shot would bring her brothers and the Paiutes. He grabbed at the pistol as she curled back the hammer. Before he could wrest the gun from her grasp, she squeezed the trigger. The hammer came down on his finger instead of the firing pin, and the next instant he landed a looping right cross that folded her senseless.

Tucking the Remington under his belt, Fargo ran to a display of various knives and laid claim to half a dozen. He ran back out, cut the ropes that bound

Cathy and Sarah, and gave the knives to them. "Free others and pass these out." There was no need to stress the urgency.

Sarah flew off the porch to Mandy and in a moment the girl was hugging her in relieved delight.

Fargo walked over to Grandma Barnes. A bright red pool had formed under her. He retrieved the Arkansas Toothpick and wiped it clean on the hem of her dress, then slid it into his ankle sheath and hurried back inside to a gun rack.

Shorty still had the Henry and the Colt, so far as Fargo knew. He needed a rifle for himself and guns for the rest of the men. Selecting a Sharps and three other rifles, he opened a drawer underneath. It brimmed with ammunition.

To lend the impression her trading post was legitimate, Granny had stocked items trading posts normally carried. With a little luck, that would help to be her clan's undoing.

Fargo hurried back out. Half the emigrants had been cut free. Parents were hugging children, husbands were hugging wives.

"This isn't over yet," Fargo said to get their attention, and shoved the rifles at Jurgensen. "Keep one for yourself and pass the rest out. There are more inside."

"Are you proposing that we fight these cutthroats?" a man named Ledbetter asked.

"Unless you want to breathe dirt," Fargo said. "They're not about to let any of us leave this canyon alive."

"Surely now that we're armed, they won't dare attack," Ledbetter said. "Especially with the army on its way. They'll flee as fast as they can."

"That's just it. The army isn't coming," Fargo enlightened him. "We're on our own." He ran from under the overhang and gazed up and down the can-

146

yon. No one was in sight but it was only a matter of time.

Ledbetter still wasn't satisfied. "You're suggesting we *kill* them?"

Everyone heard. Faces filled with fear and hope looked to Fargo for guidance. "Or they will kill you, yes."

"There must be a better way," Brickman insisted.

"Tell that to all the people they've fed to the vultures," Fargo said curtly. He was losing his temper.

Mrs. Nickelby bit her lip. "You're asking too much, Mr. Flint or Mr. Fargo or whatever your name is. None of us have ever killed another human being before."

"There's a first time for everything," Fargo said. "Or would you rather they wipe out your family and friends? Because that's exactly what they'll do." He saw indecision on a few faces. They still didn't appreciate that it could happen to *them*, even after witnessing Peter Sloane's death. He raised his voice. "You will all die. Every man. Every woman. Every child. They can't leave witnesses."

"What chance do we have?" Nickelby asked. "There are only seven of us, what with Pete dead and Jared missing. We're outnumbered, and they have those heathens on their side."

"You're forgetting the women and children," Fargo said.

"Surely you don't expect them to take up arms too?" Jurgensen asked.

"The kids, no," Fargo answered. "But your wives can help." He dashed indoors and brought out an armful of rifles and revolvers which were hastily distributed. Soon every adult, male and female, had one.

"We just stand here and wait for them?" Brickman asked. "Is that it?"

"I want all of you to lie back down." Fargo had an idea, a loco idea, but it might reduce the odds. "Exactly where you were when you were cut loose."

"What good will that do?" Ledbetter demanded. "We'll be right out in the open and they can pick us off."

"They won't shoot if they think we're still there bound and gagged," Fargo explained. "We'll let them walk right up to us, and at my signal, open fire." He glanced up the canyon but still did not see anyone. Lady Luck had been kind to them so far, but no one's luck held forever.

The emigrants were nervously looking at one another. No one had done as he told them. Then Cathy moved to where she had been lying when he cut her free and curled up in the exact same position. Sarah and Mandy imitated her example, which galvanized most of the others.

"Hurry, damn it!" Fargo growled at the few who still hesitated. He thought he had heard voices at the rear of the trading post.

Jurgensen was sinking onto the porch. "Do as he says everyone! He's our only hope of making it through this nightmare alive."

Within seconds the trap was set. They covered their rifles and revolvers with their arms and legs or hid them in their shirts or in the folds of their dresses. A casual scrutiny would not reveal anything amiss. All was as it had been except for one important detail.

Dashing to the rocking chair, Fargo carried it to where Granny usually sat. He was careful not to get any of her blood on him when he dragged her over and placed her in the chair with her head slumped to her chest as if she were sleeping. There was nothing he could do about the glistening red smear on her dress except hope it went unnoticed in the shadow of the overhang.

The voices were growing louder.

There was nothing Fargo could do about the pool of blood. He did not have the time to clean it up. So he did the next best thing. He lay so he hid the blood with his body as best he could.

"They're coming!" Ledbetter whispered.

"Quiet!" Fargo commanded, and cocked the Sharps. "No one shoots until I do. Aim for the center of their chests. That way even if you miss their heart you should hit something."

"I'm scared," Mrs. Nickelby whispered.

Someone's teeth were chattering.

Fargo was worried one of them would bolt and give it away. Then he caught movement out of the corner of his eye, and around the corner came Zeke and Caleb Barnes.

18

As Skye Fargo slid his right hand to the Remington, he swore he heard a sharp intake of breath from several of the emigrants. Zeke and Caleb didn't seem to hear it, though, and came around to the steps.

"No sign of the dirt farmer yet, Grandma," Zeke said to the figure in the chair. "The others are still searching."

"It looks like she's taking a nap," Caleb commented. His gaze drifted to Fargo, and he stiffened. "What's he doing over here? And what's that red stuff next to him?" Comprehension dawned, and Caleb snapped up his rifle, bawling, "He's loose, Zeke! He's loose!"

At a range of six feet Fargo sent a slug boring through the center of Caleb's sweaty forehead and the back of Caleb's head exploded in a shower of blood, gore, bone, and hair. Fargo fired again a fraction of a second before the muzzle of Zeke's rifle came level with his chest. He aimed for the forehead but Zeke moved and the slug cored Zeke's left eye.

Both shots echoed off up the canyon. Now the rest of the bloodthirsty pack would know something was wrong, and come on the run.

"Inside!" Fargo yelled. Rising, he sprang from the porch and gathered up Caleb's and Zeke's guns.

"Look out!" Sarah shouted.

Out of nowhere an arrow thudded into a post. Fargo spun and beheld Lame Bear and the other four Paiutes bounding toward the trading post. He snapped off a shot and brought one crashing down.

The archer was fitting another shaft to his bowstring.

Nickelby came off the porch and Fargo thrust the guns into his arms, then darted to the Sharps. A second shaft whizzed past, missing his head by inches. Fargo's answering shot lifted the Paiute off his feet and slammed him to earth.

Lame Bear and his remaining companions promptly melted into the high grass.

Only about a third of the emigrants had made it inside. Kids were pushing and shoving in near hysterics as their mothers tried to calm them and their fathers ranged along the porch.

A bellow from up the canyon warned Fargo to feed another cartridge into the Sharps and set the trigger.

"Here they come!" Ledbetter shouted.

Dix and Thorn and Swink came barreling around the bend. The moment they set eyes on the emigrants, they unleashed a blistering volley.

Lead splattered against the posts, against the wall, and into flesh. Someone screamed. Fargo fired, reloaded, and fired again. Dix and Swink were on their knees to steady their aim but Thorn charged madly, banging off shot after shot.

Some of the men dropped flat and returned fire. So did Cathy Fox.

Thorn came to a stop, squeezed off one more shot, then ducked behind a boulder, cursing luridly. "They've killed Caleb and Zeke!" he shouted to his brothers.

Almost all the women and children were now inside. Only Cathy and Sarah were left, and Cathy shoved Sarah ahead of her, saying, "Think of your daughter!"

Dix and Swink had sought cover. Along with Thorn, they were holding their fire. Or reloading, Fargo figured.

Just then a Paiute reared up in the tall grass and let fly with a feathered shaft. Fargo instantly banged off a shot with the Sharps but the warrior had dropped down. The arrow struck the wall, narrowly missing Jurgensen.

Fargo wished he had his Henry. It held fifteen rounds, not just one. Rapidly feeding another cartridge into the chamber, he backed toward the doorway.

From the vicinity of the spring came a yell. Shorty and Preston were on their way. Dixon answered them but Fargo did not quite catch what Dixon said. Jurgensen and the rest of the men had made it inside, and he followed, leaning against the inner jamb with the door wide open.

It was the only way in and out. That worked in their favor in that their enemies could only get at them from the front. But it also worked against them in that if they were hard pressed, they had no way to escape. The two windows were barely wide enough for a child to squeeze through, let alone an adult.

Dix, Thorn, and Swink were warily working their way nearer. They had plenty of boulders to hide behind and were smart enough not to show themselves for more than a second or two.

Waving stems of grass clued Fargo that the Paiutes were crawling closer, too. No sooner had he noticed than the grass parted, framing Lame Bear's vicious features. Fargo took a bead but the grass closed and the opportunity was gone.

Jurgensen and Cathy sidled to his side. The rest of the women were to the back of the room with the children, the men were at the windows.

"How long do you think we can we hold them off?" Jurgensen anxiously asked. "A day? A week?"

"An hour," Fargo set him straight, "if that." Farmers and clerks were no match for outlaws and warriors.

Jurgensen peeked out, his throat bobbing. "We can't just wait for them to massacre us."

"I agree," Fargo said. There was only one thing to do and he was the only one who could do it. Ideally, he should wait for night but the sun wouldn't set for twelve hours.

Cathy's shoulder bumped his arm. "What will they do? Rush us all at once? Or maybe try to burn us out?"

"Who can say?" Fargo replied. It depended on how much value the Barneses placed on the trading post and its contents. The thought sparked another. "There's supposed to be a root cellar here somewhere. Ask Sarah and Mrs. Jurgensen to help you find it."

Fargo raised the Sharps. Grass was moving a stone's throw from the porch. He could not see the Paiute but he had a fair idea where the warrior was, and centering the sights on the approximate spot, he fired. A swarthy figure leaped erect, clutched at his side, and reeled toward the trees.

"There's one!" Ledbetter cried, and all the men fired at once. A leaden hailstorm smashed the Paiute to earth. The grass thrashed and then was still.

A cheer went up from the emigrants. Lusty whoops and yips all out of proportion to their achievement.

Their premature crowing was nipped in the bud by a bellow from outside. "Can you hear me in there?"

"We hear you, Dixon," Fargo responded.

"Give up and we'll go easy on you."

"You've tried that before," Fargo reminded him. "It didn't work the other night and it won't work now."

"We have you trapped," Dix pointed out. "We're out front. Shorty and Preston are out back. You have little food and no water. We can sit out here until you starve, if that's what it takes."

"Be my guest," Fargo said. "But don't forget. An army patrol is due any time now." The lie had spooked the outlaws before, maybe it would spook them again. "Your best bet is to light a shuck."

"We're not going anywhere until you and those pilgrims pay for killing Granny!"

"Damn right!" Thorn cried, and rose up from behind a boulder to spray lead at the doorway and the windows.

Fargo jerked back but one of the emigrants wasn't quick enough and toppled. Some of the women and children screamed and panic threatened to spread. "Calm down!" he commanded. He had to repeat himself several times before the shrieks died down.

Jurgensen had bent over the wounded man. It was Brickman.

"How is he?" Fargo asked.

"There's a bullet in his shoulder but he should live if we can get it out."

More slugs struck the outside wall but couldn't penetrate the thick logs. Fargo turned to give Thorn a taste of lead poisoning but the wily killer had vanished.

"Fargo! Over here!" Cathy was in a far corner, beckoning. "We've found the root cellar."

A rug stitched from deer hides had covered a large trapdoor into which a metal ring had been imbedded. Cathy and Sarah had opened the trapdoor, revealing a short flight of stairs.

Fargo poked his head down in. It took a few moments for his eyes to adjust, and when they did, he was stunned. He wasn't the only one.

"My God!" Sarah breathed. "There's so much!"

Eighty wagons, the army had said. Eighty wagons full of prized possessions had been plundered by Granny Barnes and her kin. There was money, of course, and lots of it, in bills and coins. There were gold rings and gold watches and gold necklaces. There were silver rings, silver watches, and silver necklaces. Family heirlooms. Sterling silverware. China. Several clocks that had been brought over from Europe and were worth considerable money. Old books that would fetch a fine price. Granny Barnes had not missed a thing.

"It's worth a small fortune," Cathy said.

A groan diverted Fargo to the counter. Melissa was stirring. She opened her eyes as he pulled her to her feet, and immediately screeched like a wildcat and clawed at his face. Catching her by the wrist, he wrenched her arm behind her back and pushed her to the door.

Thorn popped up with his rifle trained on the doorway but he just as quickly lowered it. "Sis? Is that you?"

"Don't shoot!" Melissa shouted.

Dixon showed himself and cupped a hand to his mouth. "What the hell are you up to, mister?"

"What is *her* life worth to you and your brothers?" Fargo rejoined. "Mount up and fan the breeze or I'll kill her just like I did your grandmother." He was playing another bluff and counting on their affection for her to accomplish what all the lead in the world couldn't.

"Don't listen to him!" Melissa yelled. "I don't care what happens to me so long as you bury this bastard!"

Dixon and Thorn vanished again, no doubt to talk it over. Fargo reckoned that it would take them a few minutes to reach a decision. Enough time for him to

155

spring his surprise. "Watch her," he said, shoving Melissa at Jurgensen and Nickelby. "Shut the door behind me and keep it closed, no matter what you hear."

"Where are you going?" Cathy asked in concern.

"To end this, one way or another." Ducking low and weaving, Fargo was halfway to the west end of the porch when a Paiute yipped and an arrow whisked out of the blue to thump into a plank at his feet. His legs flying, he rounded the corner and raced to the rear. Everything depended on reaching it before the Barnes boys realized what he was up to.

A shout from Dixon gave him away. "Shorty! Preston! Watch yourselves! He's headed your way!"

To the rear rose Shorty's answering holler. "Who is?"

Then Fargo was past the trading post. He saw Preston by the fence, too startled by his sudden appearance to shoot, and he stroked the Sharps. The big rifle boomed and bucked and Preston smashed into the fence and crashed through it, a gaping hole where his jaw had been, to lie lifeless at the water's edge.

Shorty was next to the building. He, too, hesitated an instant too long, an instant Fargo used to drop the Sharps and draw the Remington. Fargo fired as Shorty drew, fired again as Shorty fired, fired a third time as Shorty staggered and fell.

The Sharps was propped again the trading post.

Discarding the Remington, Fargo reclaimed his rifle and verified a round was in the chamber. He rolled Shorty over and was elated to find his Colt. Twirling it into his holster, he spun and sprinted to the southeast corner. He had more to do yet. Six more, to be exact: Dixon, Thorn, Swink, Lame Bear, and the last two Paiutes.

Fargo burst around the side of the building and nearly collided with a painted warrior wielding a bone-handled knife. Exhibiting the reflexes of a cougar, the

Paiute slashed the gleaming blade at Fargo's throat. It was only by accident that the cold steel rang off the Sharps's barrel instead of shearing into Fargo's jugular. Pivoting on the ball of his left foot, Fargo slammed the stock against the Paiute's temple. Again the warrior sought to bury the blade in him but by then Fargo had the Sharps level and shot him in the heart.

An arrow whizzed by Fargo's ear. Another Paiute was in the high grass, nocking a second shaft with unbelievable rapidity. Just as the second arrow was leaving the string, Fargo fired. The impact spoiled the warrior's aim and put an end to his life. The shaft skimmed the top of Fargo's hat.

The smart thing to do now was reverse direction and go all the way around the trading post. Dixon and Thorn and Swink and Lame Bear were expecting him to appear at the northeast corner, not the northwest. But in the time it would take him to get there, they might move. He must act now, while he knew where they were.

Fargo charged toward the high grass. Two rifles cracked but the hasty shots missed. Launching himself into a long dive, he landed on his shoulder and rolled to the right. As he jacked up onto his left knee a shrieking demon came at him with a war club upraised to shatter his skull. He fired the Sharps once, twice, three times. At each blast Lame Bear slowed a little more. The renegade leader was only a stride away when Fargo's next shot pitched him into Paiute eternity.

Thorn was recklessly peppering the grass with lead. Dixon, ever the wiser of the pair, was holding his fire, waiting for Fargo to show himself.

On elbows and belly, Fargo wormed a dozen yards to the north and slowly rose. He could see Thorn and Dixon, both. Thorn was reloading. Dixon was scouring the grass and had not yet spotted him.

Fargo sighted down the Sharps, and when Thorn's face filled his vision, he turned it crimson with two well-placed shots.

Dixon spun, or tried to. Two more shots put a permanent end to the last male member of the Barnes clan.

Fargo scanned the boulders for Swink. Movement pinpointed the one Swink was behind. He rushed it, his finger curled around the trigger. Not until he was clear of the grass did he see Swink Gattes on the ground, the back of his head stove in by a large jagged rock. Fargo stopped dead. "What the hell?"

From behind another boulder stepped Jared Fox. "I thought you could use some help." He nodded at a thicket. "I fell asleep in there last night and didn't wake up until the shooting started. It was Melissa, you see. I was going to ask her—"

Jared said a lot more but Fargo wasn't listening. The trading post door had opened and Cathy and Sarah were flying toward him with their arms flung wide. It was a long way to the next outpost and they were bound to want to show their gratitude.

Skye Fargo smiled. He would let them.

LOOKING FORWARD!
The following is the opening
section of the next novel in the exciting
Trailsman series from Signet:

**THE TRAILSMAN #273
MONTANA MASSACRE**

*The Montana Country, 1862—
Where winters can be harsh and dangerous,
but not as much as evil men.*

The distant popping sound made Skye Fargo rein the big Ovaro stallion to a halt. He frowned, his lake-blue eyes narrowing.

That sound meant trouble, no doubt about it. The question was, would he keep riding toward it, or would he veer in a different direction to avoid it?

A faint smile tugged at Fargo's wide mouth in the midst of his close-cropped dark beard. There was also no doubt about the answer.

He heeled the stallion into a fast trot toward the source of the gunshots.

Excerpt from MONTANA MASSACRE

A cold wind blew off the Rocky Mountains in front of him, slicing like icy fingers through the fringed buckskins he wore. Fargo knew that winter was fast approaching; normally he would not have been up here in the high country at this time of year.

But a friend had asked him for help, and Fargo was not the sort of man to turn down such a request. He had stocked up with provisions at Fort Laramie and then headed northwest, into the vast, sprawling reaches of the Rocky Mountain country.

The way Washington moved the territorial lines around, it was sometimes difficult for a man to know exactly where he was, at least according to the official maps. But the people who lived up here called the place Montana, and that was good enough for Fargo. Maps didn't mean all that much, anyway, where he was concerned. Skye Fargo was a trailsman. He knew where he was, pretty much all the time.

He was on his way to an isolated Army outpost called Fort Newcomb. It had been established earlier in the year to help protect the hordes of wealth seekers who were on their way west to the goldfields in Idaho Territory. Not surprisingly, the Indians who lived in this part of the country didn't like the ever-increasing numbers of whites moving across their land.

The summons that brought Fargo here came from the fort's commander, Captain Thomas Landon. Fargo had known Landon for quite a while and had worked with him a couple of years earlier, when Fargo was doing some scouting for the Army down in New Mexico Territory.

Landon had not gone into detail in his letter about why he wanted Fargo to come to Fort Newcomb, but that didn't matter. Fargo was willing to ride up to the fort just because a friend had asked him to.

Excerpt from MONTANA MASSACRE

But now, unless he missed his guess, those shots he heard came from the vicinity of Fort Newcomb. And that meant he was riding into trouble.

Of course, that had never stopped him before. . . .

The Ovaro's ground-eating pace made the miles roll behind them. Here in the foothills, the terrain was definitely rugged but far from impassable. After a time, Fargo spotted a column of smoke climbing into the arching blue sky, which made him even more worried about what might have happened.

Down at Fort Laramie, he had heard rumors that a large band of Crow warriors under a chief known as Broken Hand had been raiding in this area. Supposedly they had wiped out several parties of gold seekers.

But with winter coming on, there weren't many prospectors traveling through the mountains in Montana, and the wagon trains full of immigrants headed to Oregon wouldn't return until the spring. Broken Hand and his warriors would have a shortage of targets to attack.

So maybe they had turned their attention to the Army post, Fargo thought grimly.

The smoke grew thicker and blacker. Fargo knew from the way it looked that it had to come from burning buildings. He rode around a bare, rocky knob of ground and found himself at one end of a long valley. At the other end lay Fort Newcomb. And just as Fargo had suspected, that was where the smoke came from.

The wind blew toward him and carried with it faint yips and shouts. Fargo quickly drew back around the knob and looked for a place of concealment. He suspected that the war party was coming right at him. It probably numbered at least forty or fifty warriors,

Excerpt from **MONTANA MASSACRE**

maybe more, and one man was no match against such odds. As much as he disliked avoiding a fight, sometimes that was the only course of action that made any sense.

He found a crevice in the side of the rocky knob and swung down from the saddle to lead the Ovaro into it. It gradually narrowed down from six feet wide at the entrance until the stone walls came together. Fargo turned the stallion around and backed the horse as far into the defile as they could go, which was about forty feet.

Then he drew his Sharps rifle from the saddle sheath and worked the lever to throw a cartridge into the chamber. He hoped the Indians would pass by without even glancing into the crevice, but if they spotted him, he would put up a fight. Only a couple of them could come at him at a time.

Unless of course they decided to stand out there and fire arrows through the opening until he was riddled. Maybe it wouldn't come to that, Fargo thought.

He heard horses coming. The swift rataplan of hoofbeats grew louder. A large party of riders swept out of the valley. Fargo brought the rifle to his shoulder and nestled his cheek against the smooth wood of the stock. He held his breath as the war party galloped on past his hiding place.

He didn't let it out until the Indians had moved on without noticing him and the Ovaro. He had caught only fleeting glimpses of them, just enough to know that his suspicions were correct. They were Crow, and he had no doubt that they were the band of marauders led by Broken Hand.

But they hadn't seen him, and so—for now at least—he was safe.

Excerpt from MONTANA MASSACRE

He couldn't say as much for those poor devils at Fort Newcomb.

Although he didn't think so, someone might still be alive inside the fort. He led the stallion out of the crevice and mounted up. The Indians were out of earshot now, so Fargo took the big black-and-white horse around the knob and toward the fort at a gallop.

Fort Newcomb was laid out on a shallow bench of ground at the head of the valley. Snow-capped peaks soared skyward behind the fort. It had been built in the square pattern that most frontier outposts adopted, with a parade ground in the center surrounded by the enlisted men's barracks, officers' quarters, post headquarters, dispensary, mess hall, barns and corrals, blacksmith's shop, armory, and storage buildings.

Several of those buildings had already burned to the ground. The others were still blazing; orange-red flames leaped high from them.

Bodies lay everywhere, their blue cavalry uniforms darkly stained with blood. Some of the troopers had been mutilated so badly that even Fargo's strong stomach rebelled a little. Others seemed untouched except for the arrows that stuck out of them like pins in a pincushion. A number of the soldiers had been shot—an indication that some of the Crow warriors had been armed with rifles.

A few horses had been killed as well, but most of them were gone, driven off by the raiders. Fargo rode slowly through the carnage that littered the parade ground, looking for any signs of life in the sprawled bodies. His face was set in hard, grim lines as he moved toward the headquarters building.

The Indians must have torched it last, because although flames licked out through the broken windows,

Excerpt from MONTANA MASSACRE

the building was still mostly intact, with the walls standing and the roof in place. An American flag flew from a flagpole in front of the building. It snapped and popped in the cold wind.

A cluster of bodies on the porch in front of headquarters told Fargo where the soldiers had made their last stand. He dismounted about ten yards from the building and left the Ovaro there, reins dangling. As he hurried up to the porch, his keen eyes searched the pile of corpses, looking for Tom Landon.

Fargo's friend was there, lying facedown across the body of another officer. Landon's hair was iron-gray, the color somewhat premature since he was only in his thirties. Fargo grasped his shoulders and rolled him over. The broken-off shaft of an arrow protruded from Landon's throat, and blood had soaked the front of his tunic.

Fargo dragged Landon away from the burning building and then went back to retrieve the bodies of the other men. It would take him a long time to bury all the dead men, but he would do it if he could. Chances were that Broken Hand and his men would not be back here any time soon.

They had already done what they came to do.

The roof of the headquarters building was on fire now, the flames leaping high. Fargo figured it would collapse soon. He bent to grab the feet of the last corpse on the porch, then froze as he heard a faint but unmistakable cry from inside the building.

Somebody was alive in there.

Without hesitation, Fargo bounded to the door, which stood half-open. "Hello!" he shouted. "Hello in there! Where are you?"

There was no reply. He shouted again, trying to

Excerpt from MONTANA MASSACRE

make himself heard over the roaring of the flames. This time, a weak voice called, "Here! Here!"

The heat slammed against Fargo's face and stole the air from his lungs. He dashed back to the Ovaro and yanked his canteen from the saddle. Using the water from it, he soaked his bandanna and tied it over his face so that the wet cloth draped his mouth and nose. Then he ran back to the porch and plunged through the door into the inferno.

Flames were all around him. They licked greedily at his hands and the part of his face that was exposed. The thick buckskins protected the rest of him, at least momentarily.

The pathetic voice had come from Captain Landon's office. Fargo whipped through the door and shouted, "Where are you?"

Smoke-wracked coughing from somewhere low down drew his attention. He looked at the floor and saw a trapdoor beside the captain's desk. It was open, and someone was struggling to climb out. Fargo bent and caught the figure under the arms. He pulled the person up from a hollowed-out place hidden under the floor.

Fargo turned, wrapping the survivor in his arms as he lunged toward the door. A blazing ceiling beam crashed down only a couple of feet to his left. He didn't shy away from it, which was good because another burning beam fell closely to his right a second later. Fargo kept going straight toward the outer door.

When he was close enough, he left his feet in a dive that carried him and the survivor through the opening onto the blood-stained planks of the porch just as the rest of the roof collapsed. Little pieces of flaming debris landed around and on top of them.

Excerpt from MONTANA MASSACRE

Fargo scrambled up and threw himself off the porch, taking the survivor with him. He rolled over and over on the ground, putting out any small fires that might have sprung up on their clothing.

He knew from the weight of the person he had rescued that it was either a woman or a child. As he blinked smoke-reddened eyes and looked over, he saw that the survivor was a woman. She wore a gray woolen dress and had long, dark brown hair worn in a single braid hanging down her back. She shuddered violently as coughing spasms went through her.

Fargo pushed himself upright and then lifted the woman to her feet. He led her over to the Ovaro. She staggered and stumbled, but his strong grip steadied her. He got the canteen again and held it to her mouth, tipping it up so that a little water ran into her mouth. She coughed and lost most of it, but Fargo kept on until he had trickled enough water down her throat to relieve some of her coughing.

Something had started to worry him. He said, "Was there anybody else in there with you?" There hadn't been time to check, and he hated to think what would have happened to anyone unlucky enough to have been caught in there when the roof collapsed.

Much to his relief, the woman shook her head. "N-no," she rasped in smoke-tortured tones. "Just me."

Fargo nodded. He ran his eyes over the woman's body, checking her for injuries. As far as he could tell, she was unharmed except for a few places on her hands and face where the flames had singed her.

She reached for the canteen again. Fargo gave it to her and let her drink as much as she wanted this time. When she finally lowered it, she rubbed her throat. It would be sore for a while, but Fargo doubted if any permanent damage had been done.

Excerpt from *MONTANA MASSACRE*

Then, as the woman looked around, she slowly lowered her hand and her eyes widened with horror. Almost everywhere she turned, lay the body of a dead cavalryman.

Fargo saw her eyes roll up in their sockets until nothing but the whites showed, and he was ready to reach out with one hand and catch the canteen when she dropped it. His other arm went around her waist to keep her from falling. She sagged against him in a faint.

Carefully, Fargo lowered her to the ground. They were far enough away from the burning building that she ought to be safe. One man had been left on the porch when Fargo heard the woman cry out from inside the building. His body was somewhat charred now, but Fargo managed to reach it and pull it away. He ignored the sick feeling in his stomach from the stench of burning flesh.

Fort Newcomb had been wiped out, the men posted here all massacred. Fargo needed only the evidence of his own eyes to know that. But the woman might be able to give him some details about what, if anything, had led up to the attack. Broken Hand must have attacked out of the blue, with little or no warning.

And when the woman got to feeling a little better, she could help him dig, too.

He went back over to her and saw that she had begun to stir. Kneeling beside her, he waited for her eyes to open.

When they did, she gasped and then started to scream and bolt up into a sitting position. Fargo caught hold of her shoulders and held them firmly. "It's all right," he told her. "You're safe now. It's all right."

Excerpt from MONTANA MASSACRE

Slowly, his words began to penetrate her stunned and violated brain. Her face crumpled into tears. Fargo pulled her against him and held her as she shuddered and wailed out her fear and anguish.

Finally she quieted, still sniffling a little as she pressed her face against his shoulder. Fargo patted her on the back, almost as if she were an infant in need of comforting.

"Are . . . are you sure they're gone?" she asked at last.

Fargo knew she meant the Crow raiders. "They're gone," he told her. "They rode off a while ago. I saw them leaving."

"But . . . they could come back . . . ?"

"They could," Fargo admitted.